BACKPACKING WITH DINOSAURS

DOUG GOODMAN

SEVERED PRESS
HOBART TASMANIA

BACKPACKING WITH DINOSAURS

This is a book about standing up.

PART 1: PREDATOR AND PREY RELATIONSHIPS

NEW PROFANITY

The rocks sang in the mid-morning air. A violent wind blew between massive rock formations, crashed into mountains, and carved draws. At the edge of one granite-rocked draw, a small hole emerged in the juniper. In the hole, a mother wolf slept with her pups. This was neither her first litter nor the first weeks of her pups' lives, so their mewling and playful pushing and tugging at her body bothered her little. She could not ignore the growling in her stomach, though. She needed the hunters to return and feed the freshly weened pups so that she could go hunting herself. Joining her would be the female beta who helped her care for the pups while the rest of the pack was away.

At the base of the mountain, one of the male wolves ran in the high grass less than a mile from his home. He had a thin black coat, yellow eyes, and a wiry frame. Like the rest of the wolf pack of New Profanity Mountain, he had descended from the mountain at sunrise, eager to hunt. Not elk or bison, no, the pack had discovered a new source of sustenance to get them through the summer: gophers.

Impractical as it seemed, the gophers were plenty from years of overpopulation, and the wolves were eager to take advantage of the gophers' complacency.

At the edge of the flat ground, the black wolf darted between several large rocks. His alpha, a large gray, snapped at him. The black wolf stopped abruptly before entering the fields. The alpha had smelled something strange in the wind, something new that none of the wolves recognized, so they tarried in the rocks, poking their heads out into the wind every few minutes to observe and learn.

The black male wondered if the new scent originated from the three legged black box, the one with the little red eye that sometimes clicked when the wolves got close. Humans put it there, and once every two weeks humans visited the clicking black box, and they left their scent all over it, but they never bothered the wolves. No, this new scent was definitely not from the box.

When nothing appeared from the forest, the wolves entered the flats. They hunted unsuccessfully all morning, chasing gophers across the fields and pouncing on their holes. It was time to employ a new strategy. So they lay down on the ground and half-dozed in the warm late-morning air.

The male kept one yellow eye half-open and directed at the hole. He slowed his breathing, and he stayed as still as possible. A tiny head popped out of the hole, looking away from him. It was only a head, so he waited. The gopher head disappeared, but a few seconds later reappeared, still not looking at him.

His muscles quivered and tightened.

The gopher crept out of the hole on all fours and sniffed the air with his little black nose.

The wolf slowly turned his head sideways, opening his mouth to reveal long, glistening teeth.

The unfortunate gopher, still unaware, stood up on his hind legs.

The black wolf shot forward. His mouth snapped shut. The gopher's back snapped in his jaws. Delicious arterial blood exploded on the roof of the wolf's mouth.

Giddy, the wolf trotted away from the kill, careful to keep the smell of the killing as far from the hole as possible. If he left scent there, the gophers would stay away from the hole for days, and he needed to eat. He gobbled the gopher down.

To his side, another pack member, using the same tactic, chased a gopher away from his hole and out into the grass where he would be defenseless and too slow for the wolf's eager mouth.

The black wolf spent the next hour canvassing the holes and devouring gophers. The last kill he did not consume but carried in his mouth. Each of the wolves were bringing home gophers to the three pups and the mother.

The New Profanity pack moved lightly through the forest and up the mountainside. It had been a good day and a good hunt. Their strategy had paid off. As long as the gophers remained in the fields, the wolf pack would survive to autumn, and then the herds of elk would return, and the circle of life would continue.

The alpha led the pack into the heavily covered forest. He was eager to return to his mate and his pups. They were his bloodline.

A sudden blur flashed in front of the pack. A yelp shattered the quiet like a scream in the dark. The hunters looked to their alpha for direction, but the alpha had disappeared. The pack froze in its tracks. Ears perked.

A bone crunched. Somewhere in the bushes, the alpha whined. The black wolf took several cautious steps toward the bushes. The other wolves followed suit. Suddenly, they saw it. Some new creature was on the mountain. It was at least as large as them, but it had eyes that dared them to retrieve their fallen pack member, eyes that gloated on the kill.

The alpha lay on the ground, his stomach disemboweled. An undigested gopher's paw hung out of the seam in the wolf's belly. At the end of the open wound was the instrument of destruction, a five-inch long claw. The other foot stood on top of the poor alpha's neck. As the wolf whined, one of the creature's toes opened like a cat's claw, slowly revealing that scimitar of a nail. It tapped on the wolf's jugular. He growled an impotent threat.

The creature waited.

The three remaining pack members growled menacingly. Lips curled, gophers dropped from their jaws, and fangs lanced the air. The wolves stood rigid and tall in the forest. The hairs on their backs bristled with fury.

And then two more Velociraptors lashed out from the side. In the blink of an eye, two more wolves disappeared into the trees. The yelping of his fellow pack members as they were killed was ungodly.

The black wolf, the lone remaining hunter, thought of the New Profanity pack up on the mountain. Two mothers and the pups remained. He could still rebuild the pack. The pups would have to be killed to ensure his bloodline, of course, but that was survival. "Of the Fittest." He was the alpha now. His bloodline was the fittest. It was up to him to keep the pack alive. Before any of that could happen, he would need to escape this moment. He considered backing away and circling the mountain to return to his pack, but in the meantime, the remaining pack members would be at risk. What if these new predators attacked the pack?

The black wolf ran the gauntlet. As he ran, the last death throes of his brothers echoed from the underbrush. He charged the hill, scared for the first time in years. He was an apex predator. He did not fear anything. He was cautious around bears and humans, but he would not admit to fear of them. This new thing, though, it terrified him. It was faster than him, and worse, it was more cunning. After he escaped, he would mark this ground to warn others to keep away. They would need to find a new hunting ground. A new apex predator had appeared.

Two shapes leaped onto the trail behind the black wolf. A little whine escaped his throat. They were so fast! He feared he would never see the pack again. The sound of their snarls reminded him of lightning crashes. Suddenly, he was knocked off his feet. Rolling onto his back, he saw a raptor stretch out to grab him with its bloody claws and flashing, bloody teeth.

The raptors sensed the wolves descending the mountains. From tree branches, they watched the wolves hunt gophers all day. With each kill the wolves made, the raptors grew hungrier and hungrier. They waited in the trees for the wolves to fill their bellies. Why kill a skinny wolf when you can eat a fat one? As evening set and the wolves returned to the forest, the raptors moved into position. When they finally decided to attack the wolves, they took them completely by surprise. The wolves tasted good as they devoured their kills. And in the air, they smelled more wolves up the draw, and puppies. Oh, good. That would come later...

7

For the past two days, the Granolas had been hiking through some of northern California's most beautiful mountains. The Perdidos stuck out like a broken sawblade cutting back and forth along the sky. Loamy smells refreshed the group every morning as they packed their gear and broke camp. As they walked along cliff bluffs, eagles whirled in the sky above like predatory acrobats. Deer and elk ambled in the morning mists, noting the backpackers' passage as if they were aliens from another planet that did not belong in this untouched land.

Caleb Henninger was content and relaxed in the wilderness. This was his element. As John Muir said, the mountains called, and he answered. Every day of the trek, he took at least a hundred photos. Caleb made sure to get up early for the sunrise shots and stay late for the night views, which were epic. On the first night, the moon had been in its vanished phase and completely nonexistent, which meant the Milky Way was a long purple cloud rising out of the mountains and stretching across the sky. He soaked it in and documented it thoroughly.

After two days of hiking, they finally arrived. Ethan led them (always the first), then silver-haired Julie, then Caleb, who was checking back on Sadie as she brought up the rear.

A giant barricade separated them from the rest of the wilderness. The large board with black zig-zags warned that the fence was electrified. Sign posts planted every twenty meters cautioned that they were approaching federal property. Not only would trespassers be prosecuted, but they'd be in violation of serious offenses.

If all those warnings felt like overkill, they were not. But here it was unnecessary. The only warning needed was the collapsed trees on the other side of the fence, and the giant claw marks twenty feet along the trunks. Caleb made sure to get a close-up shot.

"Bears can't do that," Caleb said. He was the tallest member of the Granolas, and even he couldn't come close to reaching those marks.

"How do we get in?" Ethan asked while scratching the morning shadow that was ever-present on his face.

"The door's over here," Julie Na said. She was holding up her tablet with the downloaded map. She pointed around the bend. On the far side was a small gate barely large enough for a person to walk through. A thick, coded lock on the handle prevented access.

"You sure it isn't electrified?" Sadie Fulton asked.

"I put a lot of money into this research," Julie said. "It better not be."

"That's not very reassuring," Sadie said.

Ethan walked up and touched the gate while the others shouted for him to stop. But that was Ethan for you. He was not born with the hesitance of the modern age. When Caleb and Ethan were children on the playground, Ethan was always the first kid to jump from the swing sets. When asked what he'd be when he grew up, Ethan would puff his chest out and declare that he would be an explorer one day.

Caleb unzipped Ethan's pack for the bolt cutters.

"Before we go in," Julie said, "I want to make sure everybody is ready. After this, we won't be able to go back. We're breaking so many laws right now. We'll be criminals with a capital C."

"That's never stopped me before," Ethan joked.

"That doesn't help," Caleb said with a laugh as he clapped his buddy on the shoulder.

Sadie watched her friends questioningly. Of the four, she was the least experienced backpacker, and the last to join the excursion.

Julie brushed back her silver-dyed hair and looked at Caleb. "I need this."

Caleb nodded. "In some ways, I think I've been waiting for this all my life."

Sadie offered, "Maybe you'll be able to sell the footage to National Geographic or Discovery Channel."

"I don't think they buy illegally gained footage," Caleb said, his nose scrunching up full of doubt.

"Well, there's always Instagram and YouTube then," Julie offered. "You'll be famous, Caleb."

"I'm an out of work teacher in a world where education is less unimportant than the Twitter war between Nicki Minaj and Cardi B," Caleb said. "What do I have to lose?"

"First, let's set a goal of walking back through this gate alive," Sadie said. "Then we can talk about how many different ways you all will be rich and famous."

The bolt cutters snapped the lock apart. The lock fell heavy on the ground. Julie pushed the gate open, and they walked into the world's first and only wilderness where dinosaurs roamed free.

6

"Relax," Julie said, touching Sadie's arm as they walked among the tall pines. She held out the tablet for Sadie to see. "This map of the park shows where all the dinosaurs are. It is updated every sixty seconds. See how the carnivores are all on the eastern side of the park right now? There isn't a meat-eater for five miles around us. We're safe."

"I've heard some of those meat-eaters can sniff you from five miles away," Sadie said.

"And if they move in our direction, we will know it."

Ethan added, "And if they come for us, I brought along some protection."

"What kind of protection?" Sadie asked suspiciously. "They don't make condoms for dinosaurs."

Julie and Ethan chortled.

Caleb said, "No, but the theory is that bear spray works just as well on dinos, especially the smaller ones." He handed her a canister, which she welcomed and strapped to her belt.

"Our dinosaur expert," Julie teased. "What was it they called you before we knew you?"

"The Most Awesome Man on the Planet," Caleb suggested with a curl of his lip.

"No," Sadie said, her mouth agape. "I remember. It was 'Cretaceous Caleb the Dino Nerd!'" She cackled with laughter at the memory. For a moment, her trepidations were nullified.

"Ouch," Caleb said. "I guess some things I didn't need to remember." What he didn't say was that he knew exactly what they were talking about. His memories from back then were more like nightmares, but that was before he became one of the Granola Kids.

Because of the sting of the memory, he thought about reminding them of some of their nicknames, too, but some wounds cut too deep, and he was wary of what those nicknames might dredge up. And theirs were bad, but it was nothing compared to what Sadie endured. By the age of thirteen, she first started losing pigment. It started as a little star-shaped speck under her right eye. The star grew like splotchy pale tentacles across her black skin. By the time she learned about the pigment-eating disease vitiligo, her arms and legs were losing their pigment, too, and she had refused to join any high school sports or wear anything less than full-length sleeves and blue jeans. She'd been called Patches by some kids, Oreo by the black kids, and Shit Stain by the mean girls.

"If we're bringing up nicknames," Caleb said, "I remember four names I haven't heard in a long time." Looking at Julie, Caleb said, "Isn't that right...Playa?"

Julie snickered. "MOOSE!" she cheered back at Caleb.

"And Squirrel," Ethan said in his best impersonation of the evil Russian "Boris" accent from *Rocky and Bullwinkle*.

"Don't forget Bucky!" Julie said, now holding Sadie by her arm.

That was the thing about friends. They couldn't erase the past, but they could give new memories.

"You know, maybe this isn't such a bad idea," Sadie said. "Thanks for inviting me, guys."

Julie hugged Sadie.

"Shhh," Ethan said, his tone serious. "I think I see a dinosaur."

5

The bushes ahead of them rustled as some animal moved through the undergrowth.

"You sure it isn't just a rabbit or a raccoon?" Julie asked.

One of the bushes leaned to one side.

"That's too big to be a rabbit," Ethan observed.

Caleb held his camera to his eye and began to focus.

It pushed through the bushes some more. A narrow black head with yellow teeth snarled. Everybody jumped, and Sadie screamed. The raptor screeched, showing its full row of teeth. The little dinosaur stood less than two feet tall, but it was easily four feet long with its long tail included.

After the monster finished screaming, Ethan stepped forward.

"You're kind of cool, actually," he said, not breaking eye contact. He pointed back to Julie and said, "Playa, which one is this?"

Julie checked the tablet. She zoomed in on the map. "It's not listed, actually. That's no big deal. I've heard before that some of the smaller ones aren't tracked. Or it may be a juvenile. But a juvenile what?"

"And where is Mama?" Sadie asked.

"Well, Mama isn't here," Julie said.

The little dinosaur flapped its feathered arms as it retreated up a tree, its sickle claws leaving little holes in the tree bark. The dinosaur found a perch on a higher branch. It stopped there and watched the four humans.

"I've seen this one before in zoos," Caleb said.

"Is it mean?" Sadie asked, her own fingers digging into Julie's arm.

"No. In fact, it's called Bambiraptor. You know, like Bambi."

"Bambi's sweet," Sadie said, reassuring herself.

"Yeah, so can you get your claws out of me, Bucky?" Julie asked her.

"Sorry." Sadie released her grip. While Caleb took photos, Ethan approached the tree.

"What are you doing?" Julie asked.

"I want a closer look."

"That's the stupidest thing I've heard you say today," Julie said.

"Agreed," Caleb added, "but the day is young."

Ethan removed his pack. He reached for the first branch. Once he had a secure grip, he planted a boot against the trunk and pulled himself up. The raptor protested angrily. The way it flapped its arms and shrieked at Ethan made him think of Muppets.

"If I caught him, do you think we could cook him tonight?" Ethan asked. "Has anyone here ever eaten dinosaur? I hear it tastes like chicken. Here, chickie, chickie, chickie…"

The black raptor hissed loudly and shook its tail feathers.

"That took only five seconds for you to trump your previous stupid comment," Julie said. "I don't want to know how long they'd put you away for eating a protected dinosaur."

"Only if they caught me." He reached for another branch. The Bambiraptor hopped backward.

"That's not cool, man. You don't hunt animals in the parks. Look, but don't touch," Caleb said. "I thought you were an outdoorsman. What happened to protect the environment and save the whales and all that?"

"I've never been that kind of outdoorsy person. I've hunted and I've eaten, and I've never felt any remorse about it. Besides, this is different." He reached for the final branch. His body was fully up in the tree, a large oak. "Dinosaurs were extinct once. So it's not like I'm killing an animal that has a rightful place in the ecosystem."

He lunged for the raptor. It clawed at him with its talons, but Ethan had always been very quick. He feinted, then clutched the raptor's tail as it fled farther up the tree branch. Strange blue-ribbed, black feathers fluttered around him.

"Ha! Ha!" he laughed as he held up the feathers triumphantly.

"Ethan, that's enough!" Caleb demanded. "I'm not dealing with another dead body for you. If you kill that animal, I'm leaving."

Ethan stopped his ascent. Nobody had mentioned the body in years. Not since senior year of high school.

The Bambiraptor sensed the change in the air and quieted. It raised its head as if to ask him about the dead body, too. Ethan said, "You're serious, aren't you?"

When Caleb said nothing, Ethan glanced at Julie and Sadie. They both frowned at him from behind crossed arms. "Fine, but you losers have to cook dinner tonight."

"Fine," Caleb said. "Get out of the tree."

Ethan hopped down. The Bambiraptor jumped to another pine branch and disappeared.

Ethan grabbed his pack. "Still, it was cool to see a dinosaur, right?"

The group led away from him. A somber hush, like a pall, covered them now.

"Aw, come on. Don't be like that, guys!"

4

"Dinosaur Falls National Park," Julie read from her cellphone, "was created by an act of Congress in 2020 to house formerly extinct dinosaur species created by several genetics companies. The location was determined by its remote area and varied habitats. Lands were purchased in the summer of 2020, and the dinosaurs were re-located there six weeks later. Dinosaur Falls National Park houses over 200 species of dinosaurs from the Triassic, Jurassic, and Cretaceous periods. It is strictly off limits to anyone, but the dinosaurs can be viewed through online video cameras and private lodges built around the exterior, blah, blah, blah."

"Will we be near any of the cameras?" Sadie asked as they pushed through the trees.

"No," Julie said. "The routes my company mapped out stayed well away from any cameras, or even the typical viewing areas."

"I'm sorry it didn't work out."

"I don't believe in failure," Julie said. "There were lessons learned, sure. I had a misunderstanding with my clients. I believed that if I loved the outdoors this much, so would wealthy Chinese, and they would want to come to America to have that rough outdoors experience, with a certain amount of upper class appeal. Champagne, Toyota Land Cruisers, chef-prepared meals, and all the good stuff. And I was right, they did want all of that, but not at Yosemite or Joshua Tree. They wanted what nobody else could access. So I tried, and I went bankrupt trying, but hey, I wouldn't be on this planet if not for you guys. I wouldn't be the person I am, a lover of the outdoors. A Granola."

Ethan bellowed. "I almost forgot about that name. The Granolas. Who came up with that?"

"Was it Ty?" Julie asked.

"Ty Weatherford," Ethan said. "Yeah, I think that's where I first heard it. Whatever happened to him?"

"Stanford or Berkeley, I think," Julie said.

"Didn't he go on to be a scientist or something?" Ethan asked. "I thought I heard about him in the news once."

"He's an astronaut," Caleb answered. "They have his photo displayed with a US flag that flew in space. It's in the West Lake High Hall of Fame. I walk by it every day on the way to my classroom. Well, I used to walk by it."

Ethan put his hand on Caleb's shoulder. "I'm real sorry about that, Bro.

"Yeah, well, I guess I'm out of work like everybody else."

"I'm not out of work," Sadie said.

Julie gave her a "not the time to mince words" face.

"And I was never out of work," Ethan boasted, trying to deflect the conversation away from Sadie. "Course, I was never really in work, either."

"Yeah, but your wingsuit videos have how many hits?"

"Barely enough to pay for rent, Moose. But I'm okay with that. Don't worry. You'll land on your feet. You'll all land on your feet."

"Hey, there's a dinosaur," Julie said, looking at her display. "I mean, not a Bambi thing, but like a real dinosaur. Triceratops! A herd is not a couple hundred yards from us."

"Wait, for real?" Caleb asked. "You're not playing with me, right?"

"Hey, the Playa don't play when it comes to the great outdoors. The tracker shows ten or twelve spread out across several hills. I bet we can see them over this next rise."

Ethan surveyed the area. "We will have a better view east of here, over that ridgeline." He pointed to a steep incline. "What do you think?"

"You've always had a nose for these things," Caleb said. "Let's go."

3

Getting to the top of the ridge took the rest of the morning. There were no man-made trails to follow among the Perdido Mountains. That meant they had to forge their own way until they crossed a game trail.

As they gained elevation, the sun rose and focused its rays of heat on them. Ethan removed his morning wool poncho. By lunchtime, the fleeces were back in the packs and all four were in slim athletic wear.

Sadie stopped to apply sunscreen. Being outside with no pigment was much more dangerous for her than it was for any of the others. It was the reason she had been the last to take to the outdoors. With her, there would always be a distrust of the sun.

"Is that a tat, Bucky?" Ethan guffawed, shocked. Inked on her left bicep where she had no pigment whatsoever was a majestic golden manticore with a lion's head and eagle wings. Emanating from behind it were rays in every color of the rainbow. Underneath the beast's feet read the words, *You are beautiful.*

"It's for my vitiligo, to remind me that I'm more than a disease."

Ethan traced the outline of the mythical creature with his thumb. "Why the manticore?"

"I wanted the most beautiful, colorful tattoo I could get. It's the one advantage vitiligo gives me over everybody in my family and every black person I ever knew. I was told all my life I wasn't really black because of vitiligo, but at least my tattoos could be better than theirs."

"Hell, yeah," Ethan said. But the way Caleb was looking at her, Sadie wasn't sure he was convinced. She'd seen that look on many of her accountant co-workers' faces when they'd found funny numbers that didn't make sense. Accountants were preparing to do some serious math when they made a face like that, and Sadie didn't want Caleb poking and prying. Some things she wasn't ready to talk about. So, she changed the subject.

"I have other tattoos, too. Some I could show you but some are…too personal, even for you guys."

"I get it," Ethan said. "You don't have to worry about me."

"We should get moving," Sadie said as she put away her sun block.

The hardest part of the trek was the one-hundred-yard yard rock slide. They searched for another way up, but it was the fastest route. Martens scrambled around the large rocks as the group began the ascent.

"Well, no time like the present," Caleb said, but Sadie wasn't so sure. They began the slow climb, using their hiking poles to keep them upright as the rocks slipped out from beneath them. After the first time Ethan knocked rocks down on the others as he lost his footing, they decided to ascend in a long row together rather than single file up the slide.

"And one other thing," Ethan said. He pulled a chord of belay rope from out of his pack. "We need to tether ourselves to each other. We don't want to fall back down the way we came."

Caleb asked, "Is it really so bad that we need rope?"

"I figure it's somewhere between a forty and fifty degree angle all the way up. And besides, I'm not chasing down after you when your big Moose butt goes flying down the mountain."

Caleb tied the rope to his waist.

An hour and a half later, four panting, sweaty bodies reached the summit. Sadie raised her hands up to the sky joyously.

"That deserves a beer," Julie said. "Too bad we don't have any."

"Actually," Sadie said, "I might have a little something in my pack." She shuffled through the outside pockets. "I was saving it for when we finally saw a dinosaur, but that already happened, so…"

She pulled out a flask and wiggled it in her hand. "Rum, anyone?"

"You are a dream," Julie said. After Sadie took a swig, she passed the flask around. For a moment, she felt the sting of these social situations. Often, even friends at work would hesitate to take a bite from a delicious food on her plate when they went out after work. Her dates never asked to try the food she ordered. At least, not until they asked the awkward question of whether or not her disease was contagious. It was not. But Caleb, Julie, and Ethan never blinked or hesitated. They laughed as they fought over who could have the first swig. This simple reaction made Sadie smile on the inside wider than she could ever acknowledge outwardly. She never forgot these three friends. Coming out here was the best medicine to what ailed her. This felt like coming home.

"Guys, look," Ethan said, pointing to the horizon. The frivolity stopped as the four friends gathered at the top of the ridge line. Below them was a dramatic fall of gray rocks and rich dirt, with a forest of narrow ponderosa and sugar pines. But the real view was on the fields.

In the valley below, seven Triceratops slowly moved about the high grass, using their pointed beaks to tug the grass out by the roots so that they could eat the tender parts underneath. A baby Triceratops grazed next to her mama, watching her pull out the grass, then copied her. When her juvenile beak failed to pull up the grass, the mother pulled up a mouthful and laid it down in front of the baby.

As they each grabbed their cameras, the herd approached the Seven Graves River to drink. The Seven Graves was a dangerous river full of frothing white rapids and large boulders. The narrow valleys and canyons here channeled the water into an angry torrent, but the Triceratops were not bothered by it.

An alarm beeped. Julie checked her tablet.

"What is it?" Sadie asked.

"Probably nothing. The program is supposed to alert me any time a carnivore moves within three miles of us."

Julie pulled up a screen and read the data.

"And? Don't hold us in suspense," Sadie said.

"It's the Tyrannosaur, but don't worry. It's walking around the ridge, and that's miles away from us. It's probably just following some dumb duck-billed dinosaur or something."

"You sure?"

"I've been doing this a long time, Sadie. I've participated in dozens of treks into bear and wolf country. If I thought there was a concern, trust me, I'd be the first one to get us out."

"Okay," she said, not so reassured. She didn't want anything to do with a Tyrannosaur.

"Think on the bright side," Ethan said. "If it wanders our way, maybe it will come after the Triceratops, and we'll be able to witness something nobody sees in the wild."

"I want to get closer," Caleb said. "Get some focused shots and some video of the dinosaurs."

"And I'm after a higher perspective," Ethan said. "How about we split up?"

"I'll go with Ethan!" Julie volunteered.

"Alright, Playa, you're with me," Ethan said. "Moose, Bucky, we'll see you two Granolas later."

Ethan and Julie ran up the mountain, Julie's silver hair brightening in the sun.

Before Sadie could stop them, the party had split up. She didn't like that the tablet was going away from her.

"No surprise there," Caleb said when they were alone. "Those two have been eye banging each other since we started this journey. I guess old habits die hard."

"She's emotionally scarred right now," Sadie said. "And he's never been one to say no."

"And you?"

"What about me?"

"How are you? We really haven't been able to catch up, just the two of us."

"I'm good."

"None of us are good. We're a bunch of kids who thought they'd take on the world and really mean something, and none of us made it big. We're all failures."

"Speak for yourself."

"I'm not the one with the manticore tattoo."

"Don't bring my disease into this."

"That tat has nothing to do with your disease, does it? The manticore is part lion and part eagle, kind of like West Lake High School Lions and the South Lake High School Eagles, huh?"

"I don't want to talk about it."

"I'm not going to bust your balls for this, Bucky, but don't think for a minute I don't know what you did. It may have flown past Ethan and Julie, but not me."

"Hey, you deal with the past your way, and I'll deal with mine my way."

Caleb pushed his glasses back. "Look, I'm sorry. I didn't mean to bring it up. The past is the past, and that's as it should be. Let's go find some three-horned baby dinosaurs."

He smiled warmly at her. They hugged, and then arm-in-arm they wandered down the ridgeline.

But deep down inside her, Sadie was troubled. She didn't want to talk about the Lions vs. the Eagles. She didn't want to remember the worst night of her life, even if it was also the best night of her life...

2

It was getting worse. The first time, she was shocked more than anything else, but she didn't say anything to anyone. More than anything else, she wondered how they knew the code to her locker. But this was the third time this week. She'd opened the locker between English period and "B" Lunch, and the smell exploded in her nostrils. She looked each way down the hallway, but nobody was looking at her. Felix Summer waved the air and said, "Oh, that's awful. You farted ba-ad, Patches."

She was too embarrassed to say anything. She reached in and grabbed the lunch bag. The smell was so intense, everybody watched as, head bowed and eyes locked forward, Sadie marched quickly down the hall to get rid of the bag of stink. She took it to the women's room and opened the bag over the toilet.

Plop! Plop! Plop!

Sadie gagged. She flushed the toilet and tossed the bag into the trash can. She went to the sink and washed her hands and wiped the tears from her eyes.

She remembered her last school and the kids teasing her. They'd called her names there, too. Everybody called her names wherever she went. Mama said *stick and stones, girl. You're gonna have to be strong if you going to live this life.*

Sticks and stones were one thing, but bags of crap? She could hear her mom talking to her about how hard it was making it as a black woman in America in the 70s. Life was harder back then, back when they'd sometimes be called *colored* or *your kind* or just out and out *nigger*.

"Oh my God. What is that?" Lauren said as she entered the women's room. At her side were Jenna and Kora, each one giggling harder than the other and staring at her with hawk's eyes.

Kora said, "Smells like shit in here."

Lauren smiled mischievously. She shot back, "What can you expect...from a *shit nigger*?"

They cackled at that and walked out, shouting "Don't go in there! It smells like SHIT!" Sadie fought back the tears welling up in her eyes. She looked at herself in the mirror and told herself that Lauren was a horrible racist who should just die. She wished she didn't have this stupid disease that made her so ugly and the butt of everyone's jokes. She wanted to stay in there the rest of the day, but the stench was overpowering, and people were starting to notice. There's nothing a teen-ager wants less than people to notice. So she applied some makeup she used to help blend her skin tones, and then she marched out of the restroom and off to "B" lunch.

She got in line, bought her salad because her mama warned her pizza was bad for her complexion *and that's bad enough already, girl.*

While she waited in line, she wondered how Lauren discovered her locker combination. 'Cause it had to be Lauren, she knew it. Lauren had always hated her. Sadie never knew why. But Lauren took any and every opportunity to remind her that she was a stain in her life. She stared at her reflection in the sneeze guard and hated what she saw. She remembered the image of a young, happy girl with cool black skin all over her body. She'd do anything to be that girl again instead of this patchwork monster standing on the outside looking in. The lunch lady asked her if she'd like a milk.

"Yes, ma'am."

She reached for the half pint of whole milk, and the lunch lady recoiled. She then corrected herself and smiled apologetically. But Sadie noticed she wiped her hands off on her apron after Sadie took the paper carton from her.

She faced the cafeteria room like a firing squad, with her chin up, ready for any insult. She'd need to get to the back of the room where the other losers and loners sat. She didn't look at Eric Young's table. He was the star quarterback, a handsome black man with no problems in the world who had told her once that only white kids liked Oreos. He sniffed the air as she walked past.

"Hey," somebody said from the side. She ignored them. She was done with people and insults today. She wished her Papa would just get transferred again so they could move away.

"Hey! I don't know your name."

Sadie stopped and snuck a sideways glance, her jaw set.

Three kids sitting at a table cleared a place. Two white boys (one in a Nirvana t-shirt) and an Asian girl. They wore bandanas and friendship bracelets made of paracord, and they were all in hiking boots.

"What do you want?" Sadie spat.

"We have an extra seat," Julie said. She had an ombre red dye and piercing eyes, like a falcon. She was the one who'd been calling out to her. "There's no reason to walk all the way to the back. We could use the company."

Sadie's head swiveled on her neck.

"You could wait, but everybody will just keep staring at you," Julie said.

The boy in the Nirvana t-shirt, Ethan, smiled at her. He had a very disarming smile, and a kind of Jake Gyllenhaal face. When he smiled, she knew he meant it. "Okay," Sadie said.

As soon as she sat down with her meal, Julie continued talking to Ethan, "You're crazy. Do you know how much training goes into wingsuit BASEjumping?"

"Yes, and I've watched every video I can find on it. I can do this."

"You have to walk before you can run," Caleb cautioned him.

"And birds can't fly if they don't jump from the nest. So are you going to come with me?"

"I don't know," Caleb said.

"You'll come, right?" he said, making direct eye contact with Sadie.

"Sure," she said, not knowing where this was coming from or why she was agreeing to something she didn't know the first thing about.

"No," Julie said. She put her hand on Sadie's wrist. "You can't take my girl. She doesn't even know what you're talking about. Before you agree to anything, do you know what BASE jumping is?"

But all Sadie saw was Julie's hand on her wrist. She wasn't shrinking back or recoiling. She was holding her wrist. Her hands felt cold on her wrist. But she was holding it casually, like it was no big deal. Did she know that Sadie had vitiligo? Or had she not seen? *That's impossible, Sadie,* she told herself. *Everybody sees.*

She realized the group was staring at her, waiting for her to respond. "I'm sorry. I just don't know what BASE jumping is."

"Oh, I have got to tell you about this," Ethan said. "BASE jumping is the ultimate thrill. You jump from a really high place and pull a parachute."

"That sounds scary."

"It's very thrilling, and it's the ride of your life, and next week we are all skipping school to watch me BASE jump in Yosemite."

"Yosemite? Oh, I don't go there."

"That's because you've never been."

"How do you know?"

"Because if you had, you wouldn't say that. Yosemite is the most beautiful place on earth! We camp there all the time. It has the best trails and the best views. You should come with us."

"You should totally come with us," Caleb echoed.

"Why? You don't know me."

"See, you think you don't know us, but we know you."

Her heart sank. This is where it all would go downhill. Of course they knew her. Who didn't? Whether it was *Patches* or *Oreo* or *Shit Nigger*, everybody knew her.

Ethan leaned in close to her. He smelled like pine. "We've been watching you," he said low. She bet he didn't know his voice purred when he talked low. "You're in Julie's English class."

"I am?"

Julie nodded. "Two rows back and two seats to your left."

"And Caleb says you rock in Algebra."

Caleb said, "You probably don't know that because I sit in the seat closest to the door so that I can get out of there as soon as the bell rings."

"Now, you're clearly too smart to be in any of my classes, so I've only seen you in the halls, but I trust these two, and I like the way your eyes smile."

"My eyes smile?"

"Stop it," Julie said. They finished making plans in lunch while Sadie sat back and listened to them talk in that relaxed manner like they didn't have a care in the world. She wished that one day she could be like that. Then the bell rang, and they all got up to go back to class.

Julie held Sadie back. "Look, Ethan and Caleb are two of the nicest guys you will ever meet, but they don't like being upfront about things. So I'm going to make it clear to you: kids used to call him 'dino nerd,' they wrote 'slut' on his locker, and most of my Chinese classmates call me a Banana."

"Banana?"

"Yellow on the outside, white on the inside."

"Oh," Sadie said. Her face drifted down to the table.

Julie lifted Sadie's chin. "To hell with them. He's Moose, he's Squirrel, and I'm Playa. We're the Granolas at West Lake because we like the outdoors, and that's a badge I wear with pride. I passed you coming out of English and I saw what Lauren and her Manson Family friends did. I think we have a connection and I like you. I hope you like us." She unclasped a yellow paracord bracelet and put it on Sadie's wrist. "If you're interested, we hike a lot, we camp sometimes, and we eat lunch together."

Julie smiled and ran off to class. Sadie looked down at the bracelet wrapped around her wrist. A ghost of a smile tugged at the ends of her lips.

1

It was strange how little Sadie's life had changed in the few weeks that had passed since she met the Granolas. She was still this shy girl who was reluctant to speak out in class or talk to others. People still looked at her differently and often stared. To most of her classmates she was still a freak of nature. They continued to treat her as diseased, even though vitiligo could neither harm nor infect them.

At least once a week, a bag of dog crap appeared in her locker. Julie helped her get the locker combination changed, but that didn't stop the "phantom crapper," as the Granolas took to calling this person. Nobody had figured out the phantom crapper's identity, in part because the lunch bags appeared at different times of the day: sometimes after gym, sometimes before lunch, and once the bag was delivered after the last class bell. They knew this because Sadie only discovered it after going back to her locker for final home changeout. (She was *so* thankful it didn't stew overnight.) As best they could guess, it was somebody with access to the school files because they knew the old number and the new one.

For all that had not changed, a monumental shift had occurred in her life. Her friends took her hiking and camping, and she even skipped class to watch Ethan's first flight in a wingsuit. To everybody's surprise (everybody's except his own), Ethan survived the flight and posted the video online. The next day he was the talk of the cafeteria, and people didn't seem to mind that she was there.

They still called her Patches and Oreo, but she didn't mind as much because she had friends who accepted her for who she was. It wasn't that she was beautiful in their eyes, but that she was just another person, and ever since the day the little star first appeared beneath her eye, that was all she'd ever wanted to be.

Homecoming changed everything.

Ethan and Julie had been dating since right before Sadie met the Granolas, so it went without saying that he would ask her to Homecoming. And even though she didn't expect it because she'd never been asked out before, she still had hope that Caleb would ask her. It wasn't because she expected him to find her attractive, and it wasn't because she liked him that way (but she did a little), but it made logical sense. Ethan and Julie would go, and they'd want their friends with them. It would be more fun that way. He was single, she was single. It worked.

But the thing was, Caleb never asked her to Homecoming. Fifty times in the weeks leading up to Homecoming, she thought of ways to ask him out. Twice she almost got there, but every time, something got in the way.

The Monday of Homecoming Week, she obsessed about it all morning. It completely occupied her mind. She couldn't concentrate on anything but running through the scenarios in her head. She had decided on the straightforward approach rather than the joke version of "so, Homecoming, right? That's still a thing?"

She stared at him all during Algebra. He stared at the open door. She needed an opening, a moment when it was just the two of them. She tried to catch him after Algebra, but he bolted for the next class without a word.

Teen lust gave her the opening she'd been looking for. Julie and Ethan had been hitting it heavily since his wingsuit stunt on his birthday. Julie confided in Sadie that Ethan was now officially her first, which she was fine with. There was something rebellious in her first not being a Chinese boy. She still planned to marry Chinese one day because that's what her parents wanted/demanded, but until then she was enjoying her time with Ethan.

So when Ethan and Julie excused themselves to go the bathroom with about five minutes left in Lunch, Sadie knew the real reason was to go find a place to make out or bone, though she liked to think Julie wasn't the kind of person to "bone."

As soon as they left, Caleb and Sadie asked each other something at the same time.

"Could you mentor…"

"Do you want to go"

"…me in Algebra?"

"to Homecoming with me?"

"Wait, what?" she then said. Her cheeks flushed under her makeup.

"I'm sorry," he said. "I can't."

Her eyes got blurry, and his face flushed. "I'm sorry. I have to go," he said, collecting his tray and walking off.

"Wait," she said. But he didn't. He kept walking.

Sadie was crushed. She grabbed her tray to take it to the trash cans. Lauren and her friends were at the table behind her, snickering. Eric Young had his arm on Lauren's shoulder, and he was laughing, too. So were two of his friends from the football team.

"Nobody dates trash, and they sure don't go out with them when they smell like shit, Shit Bag," Lauren laughed. The others laughed hard like Lauren was the cleverest person in the world.

"Go to hell," Sadie whispered under her breath. She didn't realize she'd said it. She thought she'd just said it using her inside voice, but it came out all the same.

Suddenly, the group's demeanor changed. Lauren jumped to her feet. "What'd you say, Shit Bag?" She pushed Sadie backwards. Sadie immediately hunched over.

"That's right. You don't get to talk to me like that. You don't get to talk to me AT ALL!"

Sadie walked out.

"You better walk away, or next time I'm going to stomp your ugly ass, Shit Bag!" Lauren yelled. Two teachers approached Lauren, and she told them Sadie was calling her names, which was why she called her a Shit Bag. They didn't believe her.

Caleb texted her that he wanted to talk. She ignored him. She was a pro at ignoring people. She could ignore him, too.

He e-mailed her before class was out. The bolded message preview glared at her like hazard lights around a Do Not Enter sign. She right-clicked on the message and slid the cursor to "Delete," then moved it to the folder labeled "Granola." Once there, the "Granola" folder blipped into bold font. She sighed and closed her e-mail.

After school, she went straight to the library rather than wait for the bus. She called her mama and told her she had missed the bus for tutoring after school. When Mama picked her up in the Mazda hatchback, she studied her daughter peculiarly.

"You've never stayed late for tutoring before," Mama said before turning the car on.

"Can we just go?"

"That's a lot of attitude, girl."

"I'm sorry, Mama. I don't feel well. Can we go?"

Though her maternal instincts didn't trust Sadie's rationale, she drove her daughter home.

At 7pm, the doorbell rang.

"Probably some kid selling us coupons for football or soccer or some useless garbage," Papa groused to Mama. "Tell them I don't need another half-off Fridays at Casa Frijole."

Mama opened the door. Caleb stood there sheepishly.

"I'm not buying another coupon book," Mama said.

"Is…is…Sadie home?"

Mama's eyes went wide.

"Can I speak to her? It's important."

"Sadine?" Mama called out. "There's a white boy out here who calls you *Sadie*." She emphasized the name in the whitest way possible. "Why?"

Sadie growled at her mother to be quiet. Mama growled back that she'd be as loud as she wanted in her own house, *Sadine*.

Sadie poked her head out from behind the mostly closed door.

"Can I talk to you?" Caleb asked.

"I don't want to talk to you."

"Please?"

"There is a boy who wants to talk to you. Talk to him," Mama said in her fiercest hushed voice.

Sadie waved her off. She stepped outside and closed the front door behind her.

"What do you want?" she grumbled.

He opened and closed his hands. "Look, I'm sorry. I was stupid. I was nervous, and I ran off, and I shouldn't have done that. I heard you and Lauren got in a fight."

"No, she just barked a lot."

"I'm sorry. I should have been there."

"You say you're sorry a lot but I don't know what for. We're just kids who share lunch together."

"And Algebra," he added. She fixed him a serving of icy stare cold enough to give him brain freeze if he ate it.

"So, the reason I can't go with you is that somebody already kind of asked me. I mean, they didn't ask me ask me. It's more like an agreement. I sound like an idiot."

She raised her eyebrow.

"Every year for Homecoming I have an agreement to take my cousin, Madison, to the dance. We don't usually hang out that much. She has other friends, and even a boyfriend that my aunt and uncle don't know about, but since they don't know about it, I have to get dressed up and take her every year. It is miserable. I sit around and drink stupid punch for an hour because we always have to be the very first people there. Then Ethan and Julie show up and we go hang out."

"So you can't go to Homecoming with me because you're dating your cousin?"

"I am NOT dating my cousin," Caleb quickly retorted. Then, more slowly, he continued. "I am *chaperoning* her. There's a difference."

Sadie giggled. "You're dating your cousin!"

"Stop saying that!" he said, a little hurt. She could tell this was a sore spot for him, but she knew he could take it. She felt about a million times better, if you ignored the part where she was dumped because a guy was dating his cousin.

"Sadie, will you go to Homecoming with me?"

"But, your cousin?" she asked without a hint of sarcasm.

"I can pick you up after I get her. Trust me, we leave early enough as it is."

"I don't know."

Mama yelled from inside, "Say 'yes!'"

Sadie whipped around. Her parents were watching from the dining room window with the curtain pulled back. Her Papa was eating popcorn. Popcorn!

Sadie pointed back to Caleb. "He's taking his cousin to Homecoming."

"I heard," Mama said. "I don't care."

"Go away!"

"Sadie," Caleb said. "I'd really like it if you'd make Homecoming something that isn't completely miserable and boring. Please, would you go with me?"

She smiled out of the corner of her mouth and said, "Fine."

It turned out Madison was very nice, and seeing Caleb grimace around her was totally amusing. He drove, and Madison had already moved to the back seat by the time they picked up Sadie.

They drove in awkward silence for five or six blocks. Caleb may have been reviewing ways to kill himself out of embarrassment, but Sadie was thinking about all the things Mama had told her about boys and first dates, even though Sadie told her a thousand times that this was not a first date. Madison watched the awkward silence for as long as she could take it, then blessedly intervened on their internal musings with her own explanation of the night because the story went deeper than Caleb had previously let on.

Madison was gay, but her parents didn't know that. She didn't want them to know, either. Not everybody in California was down with gay pride. So Maddy was dating Claire, and Caleb had actually gone on three dates with Maddy so that her aunt and uncle remained in the dark.

"Caleb, you are such a sweetheart," Julie said at the table.

"Please don't mention this to anyone, and stop saying I dated my cousin."

Julie pointed to Maddy and Claire, who were dancing together. "It makes sense that Maddy doesn't want her parents to know," Julie said. "My parents don't know about Ethan."

"They don't?" Ethan said.

"They do not want their Chinese daughter dating a white kid. They already have to deal with a daughter who doesn't speak fluent Mandarin, dyes her hair ombre, and wears hiking boots."

"What about your parents?" Julie asked Sadie. "Do they care that you went to Homecoming with a white kid?"

"Are you kidding? They practically pushed me out the front door. Have you seen me? This," and she emphasized her whole body, "isn't dateable material."

"I'd date you," Ethan said. Julie raised her eyebrows jokingly at him.

"Seriously. You're smart and you're funny, and I know we don't talk about it or whatever, but I think your skin looks beautiful."

Sadie's heart wanted to melt.

Julie agreed. "You are beautiful, Sadie."

"You are," Caleb chimed in. "And you are my date tonight. Let's dance."

After the second set, they took Homecoming pictures. Sadie couldn't wait to show them to her mama.

They danced some more, switching partners for the slow dance so that Julie and she could dance with somebody who didn't have two left feet, and so that Caleb and Ethan could take the opportunity to waltz around the gymnasium like they were competing on Dancing with the Stars. They were apparently too convincing because the biology teacher told them they made a cute couple and it was about time Ethan came out.

Then it was time for the Homecoming King and Queen to be announced. Lauren was the announcer. Ty Weatherford, future astronaut, was obviously the Homecoming King. He got a golf clap from the Granolas, who were all a little jealous of him. But when Lauren called "Sadie Williams," nobody could believe it, especially not Sadie. She walked up to the end of the gym floor as Queen's *We Are the Champions* blared over the loud speakers.

In front of everyone, Sadie got nervous. Two large paper bags sat at Lauren's feet. She told herself to just walk away, but she couldn't stop.

"For the King," Lauren said, and she pulled a plastic crown out of the bag and placed it on Ty's head. He held his hands up while everyone cheered, then he stepped back to give Sadie the spotlight.

"And for the Queen on this day when the Lions beat the Dragons," Lauren said to a rousing cheer. She looked Sadie square in the eye as she slowly leaned down to the bag. She reached in, and Sadie tensed.

But then Lauren pulled out a shiny tiara with Swarovski crystals and lifted it high for everyone to see. "All hail the Queen!" Lauren said as she placed the glittering tiara on Sadie's head. She whispered into Sadie's ear, "Shit Nigger."

Lauren didn't turn off her mic. People didn't clap or cheer. Ty's face was a mask of shock and horror.

"Dammit," Lauren said. "Wait," she added, suddenly remembering something. She jumped back.

A bucket of fresh cow manure from the stockyards dropped from atop the stage rafters. Sadie's eyes darted up at the last second, but she was paralyzed. Caleb, who ran up to the stage as soon as Lauren dropped the N word, yanked Sadie aside. She narrowly escaped being covered head to toe in animal waste.

1.5

The foul waste lay like bile on the stage. The crowd remained in a semi-catatonic sense of shock. Then Principle Matthews stepped forward. He took the mic from Lauren and tossed it on the floor.

"Caleb, escort Ms. Sadie outside and get her some water." He nodded to two teachers, who moved to meet Caleb and Sadie. Ethan and Julie were already there.

To Lauren, he said, "You. Come with me."

"But," she said.

"No. You're done here." He took her by the arm and led her offstage and out of the gym.

Within minutes, the gym slowly emptied. Students drove away in a silent and sullen stigma. Lauren's parents were called. She was immediately suspended until further notice. Principal Matthews explained that this was only the beginning, and a full investigation was under way.

Sadie didn't cry. She wiped away the start of tears and stood outside. She didn't talk to the Granolas, and they didn't have much to say either. Sadie's parents came and picked her up.

Sadie didn't go to school the next day, even though her parents told her she was making a mistake. She had to get back on the horse and ride it, Papa said. To her mother, though, staying home from school was giving in to the racist bullshit. Now was the time to be a proud black woman, push her shoulders back, and walk through the halls at school like she owned them. Sadie wasn't ready for it.

Caleb came over after school. Sadie saw him through the kitchen window. He pulled up in his old Honda Civic. She was walking to the door when he gently knocked, but her Papa headed her off.

"You can't talk to that boy," Papa said.

"But he's my friend. I want to." Papa glared at her until she took a step back. Caleb knocked again, with a little more force. She couldn't hear all the words when her Papa chased him away.

"Ain't nobody okay after a thing like that," she heard her Papa say to Caleb. She really wanted to talk to him, and Caleb sounded awful.

"Go away, son. Go home."

She watched him walk back down the walkway to his car, shoulders slumped. She wanted to cry.

Papa closed the door behind him.

"Why won't you let me talk to him? He just wants to help."

Papa shook his head in disgust.

"But he's my friend."

"Him? Sadine, don't be stupid. A boy like him thinks he can extend a hand and pretend like it's all Kumbaya and roses. But he don't live it. He wakes up every morning, and he's a white kid living in a white world, but not my girl. When you wake up, you're a black woman, and nothing *your friend* can do or say will ever change that."

"Why can't I talk to him, though?"

"'Cause baby girl this has been building up for years. You don't fight. And because you don't fight, you're practically asking people to belittle you. You need to learn to live in this mean-ass, racist world without a crutch. Do you think when I was growing up in the 60s and 70s, people didn't call me a nigger? I grew up on the border between Mississippi and Alabama! If the worst thing that happened to me was some kid called me a nigger, that was a good day. I had friends that were tied up and…."

He stopped and stared at Sadie for a moment, his eyes wet with tears. "Racism, bullying – it's all the same thing. Hatred served up in a different recipe. And it's nothing new. This is 2004. Racism was there in Roman times, in Neanderthal times. It probably crawled up out of the water when the first toad decided he didn't like the look of another toad just 'cause he was darker than the other. It's primordial. So something that old, that ingrained in people, where will this Caleb kid be when you're in college and some frat boy calls you a hood rat? Where will he be when the kids down the street call your kids Oreos because of the color of their mama's skin? Sadine, you've got to learn to make it on your own."

2

Julie remained close to Ethan as they hiked up to the higher ridge line. He still smelled like she remembered, of pine and earth and burnt timber, and faintly of his devotions to green tea and M&Ms. Once upon a time, she had been seduced by those smells and the life they promised. Ethan was a lost cause, though, a boy who never grew up, and as such, completely unsuitable as a partner.

But here, in this magical land where dinosaurs thrived, maybe there was something more.

He took her by the hand and led her to the cliff's edge. A gray stone face fell to the ground and sloped outward into the valley. On the opposite side of the valley rose a second ridge line, this one jagged and dangerous. In the distance, a forest fire's smoke bloomed like an ugly flower that darkened the setting sun. This wasn't the most beautiful place in the park – that would be the eponymously named Dinosaur Falls – but it was a close second in her opinion.

"It was created by a glacier eons ago," Ethan said as he removed his pack and pulled the wingsuits out. "But the funny thing is, the dinosaurs are older than the glacier."

"Wow. You are full of great trivia," Julie said.

"I can't take credit for it. Caleb told me about it. He said most of the dinosaurs are at least as old as the Rockies themselves, and some of them are older."

"Well, still. It's good to hear. The Perdidos are beautiful. Is that an Ankylosaurus?" Julie reached for her binoculars. There was something large and low moving along the valley floor, but she wasn't sure exactly which dinosaur.

Ethan handed her a green and blue helmet. "Let's go find out."

Twenty minutes later, they finished donning their suits and safety checking them. Julie used the GPS locator on her tablet to mark the location of their packs, which they raised high into the trees.

"Do you think that will keep them safe from dinosaurs?" she asked.

"Well, it's about as high up as I can get them, so it will have to do. Besides, we won't be too long. We will come back for them tomorrow."

Julie didn't like the idea of hiking back up the ridge just to gather their packs, but at the same time, she was eager to wingsuit again. She'd flown several times to collect footage that she hoped would entice clients from China. That hadn't worked as well as she had hoped, but she got some kick ass experiences out of it.

"The suit fits perfectly," she said.

"It should. It's your old one from high school."

Julie's mouth dropped into a bowl shape.

"I had no idea this thing still existed. I forgot all about it."

"Well, never let it be said that I'm not sentimental. You ready?"

"Oh, yeah."

He made a grand gesture with his arms and said, "Ladies first."

She chortled. "Um, okay, doofus. Like you're some gentleman." She tucked the tablet into her parachute pouch and walked to the very edge of the ridge. She took a moment and mentally pictured the flight. This was technically BASE jumping with a wingsuit, and very, very risky. But she had inspected the wingsuit thoroughly. Now she envisioned herself soaring along the wall and out over the valley. With any luck and heat rise, they would land along the far side of the valley.

Julie took several deep breaths. In so many ways she was the baby chick on the edge of a nest preparing to fly, flapping her arms so that she could see the wings fan out. Once she was certain of their rigidity, she leaped into the air and dove to the ground below.

The rocks slid in a blur beneath her. The air sung around her face. As she spread her arms and legs outward, she felt the shudder of the wind catching in her unfurled wings. It was a momentary zip followed by a slap of air, and suddenly she was flying along the side of the valley.

She zoomed along the side briefly. She wasn't here to rush over rocks and trees. She could do that anywhere. Today was all about flying over dinosaurs.

Julie fanned out into the valley. The summer rage created a strong updraft that kept her flying much longer and farther than she had expected.

Her goal was the Ankylosaurus. She flew over the giant armored tank of a dinosaur, its bold studs and horns hiding its tender belly. She was reminded of a horseshoe crab. A giant, monstrous-sized horseshoe crab with a pulverizing club at the end of its tail.

Two smaller Ankylosaurus babies walked behind the mother, their bodies tucked close to the mother's armor. Julie wondered if the behavior had ever been observed before, which made her glad that she had her helmet cam on, recording every microsecond.

Maybe this is the change I need, she thought. *Maybe I can turn this footage into profit, maybe start a YouTube channel and then use that seed money to start a media company, an empire.* She just had to figure out who her audience was and what they wanted. That was the only trick. Flying like Supergirl over the vast land of primordial creatures, she felt confident that her life would change for the better.

She coasted over a flock of Edmontosaurus hadrosaurs, each the size of a moving van. They slowly walked along the valley to Seven Graves River.

"WOOHOOOOO!" she cheered, not that the dinosaurs could hear her at this height. (Or so she thought. Maybe one or two of them scanned upward in her direction, wondering what was up with the weirdly-acting pterodactyl.)

She felt a rush of positive energy coursing through her body. She felt more alive than she'd felt in months. In the back of her head, the image of a sad Julie with tears in her eyes filing bankruptcy papers echoed out to her. That had been the bottom of the fire pit for her, nothing but ash and smoke and depression in every direction. Every day was an uphill climb to force herself out of bed. Then she had to downsize to a new apartment. It was one emotional and embarrassing battle lost after another. Truth be told, she was two months away from moving back in with her parents, and she did NOT want to do that. Without the extra food rations she'd purchased for expeditions, she'd be going to the homeless shelter for food. Until then, she drank champagne and ate lots of dumplings, and she harbored a hope that life would get better.

That small nugget of hope was magnified a hundred thousand times by the adrenaline rush of this jump. Julie smiled uncontrollably. Then she laughed like she hadn't laughed in a long time. The beauty, the rush, it all surged through her.

She reached behind her back with both arms and pulled the cord, deploying her chute. The parachute popped out of her pack and snapped taught. Momentarily, the parachute pulled her back upward before she began her descent to the ground.

She landed, running and jumping and waving her arms. The ridge lines seemed so massive and impeding from the bottom of the valley.

Ethan floated to the ground behind her. Julie all but jumped into his arms as she hopped up and down in joy.

"Can you believe that?" she asked.

"Did you see the duck-billed dinosaurs?" Ethan shot back. He was as blown away by the flight as she had been.

"The Ankylosaurus family?" she responded. "There was a mama and she had two babies and it was maybe the most amazing thing I've ever seen in my life!"

And then she was pulling his face down to hers. She didn't remember thinking about it. She just decided right then and there that this moment needed a kiss, and Ethan was a good-looking guy. She pulled him down to her, and he embraced her fully, pulling her up off her feet and twirling around. But in all the excitement and twirling, he almost got her tangled in his chute.

He immediately dropped her back to the ground, both of them laughing. They spent the next minute collecting their chutes and repacking them.

"I can't wait to tell the others," Ethan said.

"I can't wait to see the footage. I have some ideas. I think this is going to change everything."

"Always a play, Playa? Don't ever change."

They kissed again, and for a moment she thought about taking this a little further. It had been a long time since she'd been with anyone. She'd been too preoccupied with starting (and driving into the ground) a business to pursue boyfriend status with anybody. And this was no time to start a serious relationship. But a moment's dalliance? (She rolled her eyes as she thought of a dalliance, like she was some Victorian age girl. Side hustle, maybe, but *dalliance*? That wasn't her and never would be.) Julie thought about it more. She thirsted for Ethan. Like vintage Hollywood cowboys traversing a massive desert and singing of the prospects of cool water, her body thirsted for his. She went in for another drink of his lips.

But Ethan's face twisted away from her. She followed his eyes. The rush of the adrenaline had taken over her hearing. It was returning to her like the clap of an ocean wave. She heard a motor. A cloud of dirt rose from the grass in the distance.

3

The truck slammed to a stop in front of Julie and Ethan. It was a strange hybrid of pickup and dune buggy. Ethan thought it would be equally capable in the desert as the arctic. He also noticed the heavy armor plates bolted to the roll cage. The plates were scuffed but not dented. Ethan wondered what kind of animal encounters this vehicle had faced.

Julie backed away from him as the door of the Raptor opened, which would have soured his mood if he didn't know from experience that Julie could be hot and cold that way. When she was alone, she wanted her lovers close, but as soon as some new stressor approached (like one of their teachers or Erik Younger), she pushed him away.

"We're dead," Ethan grumbled.

The door to the truck opened, and out stepped a park ranger. The man wore pleated pants that Ethan suspected were more durable and rugged than they implied. His moustache was streaked with white hairs like rain in a black and white movie. The crow's feet around his eyes were more like the feet of an ostrich. He was talking into a brick-sized radio with a long antenna as he exited his truck.

"I've got them," the park ranger said into the radio. Ethan couldn't hear what the other park ranger was squawking back over the radio.

"Don't say anything until we know what he wants," Ethan mumbled to Julie. She nodded. This wasn't her first time on the wrong side of the law.

The officer didn't waste time. "Get in the truck," he said.

"Did we do something wrong?" Ethan asked.

"You did about half a million things wrong, son, and you broke at least half a dozen laws doing it, but right now that isn't my concern. I need to get you to safety."

"Safety?" Julie asked. She started to mention the tracker, then thought better about it.

"Yes, ma'am. If you had BASE jumped in any other direction, you'd be a lot safer, but no, you dumbasses flew the length of the valley. Now you're less than 500 yards from a T-Rex, and upwind of him, too. You might as well have doused yourselves in barbecue sauce, too. Now come on. T-Rexes have one of the best noses on the planet and can smell prey from more than five miles away. And once they get something in their noses, they don't stop until they've finished their trail. We have to go. Now!"

Ethan felt a cold ball forming at the base of his spine. As an adventure junkie and outdoor enthusiast, he hadn't felt that cold ball often. He could probably count on one hand the number of times he'd felt it in his life, but he trusted his instinct. He didn't need to be told twice to get out.

At the same time, a proximity alarm blared from the truck's console.

The ranger cursed. "Move it!" The park ranger jumping back into the truck scared Ethan and Julie more than anything else. His passenger seat was full of gear, so they leaped into the truck bed.

"I wish I could clear room and get you buckled, but we've got to haul ass," the ranger barked. "This'll be bumpy. Hold on tight."

The ranger shifted the truck into gear. At the same time, a giant head with sinister eyes and large teeth emerged from the forest.

"Oh, man. That's a T-Rex!" Ethan shouted.

"How did we get so close?" Julie asked as she pulled out the tablet.

"Hurry!" Ethan shouted to the park ranger.

The Tyrannosaur shoved through the undergrowth below the trees and sprinted at them.

The wheels of the truck spun, and it jumped forward, nearly throwing Ethan and Julie out of the truck bed. Julie screamed. The tablet bounced to the end of the truck bed and rattled against the mesh net tailgate.

Ethan grabbed the roll cage.

The T-Rex crossed the distance between them in three quick strides. Her head shot forward like a rocket, as the truck swerved to the side. The jaws snapped close enough to Ethan's face that he could feel the heat in the dinosaur's breath.

The T-Rex didn't give up the pursuit. She was now using her giant feet to reach out and stomp the hybrid to a stop. Each clawed step barely missed the rear bumper of the truck, which bounded over the valley floor.

"Don't you have a faster gear?" he yelled at the park ranger.

The truck accelerated. The T-Rex's head cocked to a 45-degree angle, as if she was considering this new development. Then she took one step and leaped into the air at the truck.

Julie and Ethan screamed as ten tons of flesh and bone crashed down on them. Giant claws flexed.

The T-Rex landed with enough power to snap the truck's axle and impale it into the ground. By some miracle, Julie and Ethan avoided being pinned under the T-Rex's claws. In a state of shock, they didn't move. A part of Ethan thought that if he didn't move, maybe the T-Rex wouldn't notice him.

The front wheels stopped, and the powerful Tyrannosaur roared his warning to everyone else in the world that this was her kill. Her roar sounded like a heavy metal concert being interrupted by the attack of a thousand hungry bald eagles. It was a weird mix of Angus Young and Dimebag Darrell that Ethan had heard only once or twice before on television shows but would now never forget. The power of the T-Rex's air sacs was overwhelming.

The park ranger, covered in his own blood, stumbled out of the truck. He carried a heavy, giant-barreled pistol in his hand, which he raised into the air. He was about to shoot it when the T-Rex snatched him up in her mouth. The T-Rex shook the park ranger from side to side. With his last ounce of energy, or perhaps as his final death twitch, the park ranger fired the pistol.

It sounded like a firecracker going off. The T-Rex shrieked, dropping the remains of the park ranger and running away.

Ethan and Julie hugged each other tightly in what was left of the truck bed.

"I want out of this truck," Julie said suddenly.

"Good idea." They both hopped over the side.

What was left of the park ranger was a bloody pulp in the fading light. The lower half of the man's body could be easily distinguished, and Ethan had a profane thought about how the man's pleated pants held up really well in the mouth of the Tyrannosaur. He felt bad about that thought and dismissed it from his head.

Except for the arms, the upper half of the man's body was mush. He thought a piece of the man's rib cage poked out in the wrong direction, but he couldn't be sure. One hand still held the pistol.

Suddenly everything in Ethan's stomach had to get out, and he hurled it into the grass.

"What just happened?" he asked, spit dribbling from his chin.

"We nearly got eaten by a dinosaur," Julie tried not to scream. "We need to get out of here." She ran to the back of the truck bed to check for her tablet. It wasn't there, so she got on her hands and knees and searched the ground around the truck.

Ethan pulled the pistol out of the dead ranger's hand and grabbed Julie by the arm.

"Hey," he said.

"We can't go. I have to find that tablet. It tells us where all the dinosaurs are, Ethan. You understand what I'm getting at? The predators, Ethan."

"Right. That's a good idea, but look."

She turned around. The T-Rex stood maybe a hundred yards away, shaking her head. Every once in a while, she would glare at them nastily, take a step, and then shake her head again.

"You saw how fast that thing moves," Ethan said. "We need to leave now."

"But we're dead if we can't track them or use the map."

"Julie!" he yelled in as hushed a voice as he could manage. He pulled her away. The T-Rex had taken another step toward them.

They ran off into the grasslands, trying to put as much distance between them and the mighty T-Rex. Before they ran off, though, Julie stopped and grabbed the ranger's radio out of its console.

4

Caleb followed Sadie down into the valley along the river's edge. They took their time going around the rock slide on this side of the ridge. Neither of them were as adventurous as Ethan or Julie, so they were happy to take a slower pace as they descended into the valley.

While Sadie stopped to make some field notes, Caleb set up a tripod and took more photos of the Triceratops. He couldn't get over their horns. What he'd seen in footage just didn't do them justice. There was rarely a frame of reference to how big these beasts were. They dwarfed the bison he'd photographed in Yellowstone, and those bison had been huge and imposing beasts.

Sadie touched his bare arm. He felt the warmth of her skin, and it gave him a chill. There was something electric there, but was it because of their past, or something else?

"Look," she said, pointing to the valley.

Antelope crossed into the meadow next to the Triceratops.

"They're working together," Caleb said. "It is a new twist on prey relationships. It's called a perpendicular prey relationship because…"

"Parallel would be between two non-extinct species."

"Exactly." Then he added, "I'm sorry. Sometimes the teacher in me comes out."

"It's okay. That was actually a lucky guess. Biology was never my favorite class. I left that to you."

"Hey, I still say I wouldn't have passed Algebra if not for all those Tuesday study sessions with you."

"Yeah, you really sucked."

They both laughed. She had a beautiful laugh. She was always reserved, always assuming people would say the worst about her, and who could blame her? Many had. From his experience, all of Sadie's life had been fitted into this specifically horrible place where everybody had an opportunity to tease her. Blacks because she was white. Whites 'cause she was black. And then there were the overwhelming majority who assumed she was sick or contagious. It disgusted him anytime he encountered it, and like Julie and Ethan, they always stepped in to stop even the slightest suggestion of the bigotry. She had always been that person for them, the protected one who brought them together. Of all four, she was the one best known by her nickname, Bucky, because it was so important to who she wasn't.

His heart must have been on his sleeve because she changed the subject. "So tell me more about perpendicular prey relationships."

"Sure, Bucky. So, the Triceratops rely on the antelope to tell them when a predator is nearby. But the predators in Dinosaur Falls are just not interested in a tiny morsel like an antelope. A T-Rex needs something bigger."

"Like a Triceratops, which is the size of a small tank."

"You got that right. But it's not the most interesting part," he teased.

"What's that?"

"It's the predator relationships. This area, like much of northern California, was the home to mountain lions, bears, and wolves. But once the dinosaurs were moved in, they all disappeared. The apex predators of our world were dethroned by the apex predators of their world."

"Wait, so there are no bears here?"

"A bear may feel like he can eat anything, but when the T-Rex comes around, the bear is just another meal. Whereas the antelope may go unnoticed, the bear does not. Raptors chased off wolves, and mountain lions and bobcats left next. As a result, Dinosaur Falls has more non-extinct prey animals than ever before."

"Won't that destroy the land, though?"

"It would, but the park is constantly being transformed. Hadrosaurs and Triceratops prefer conifers and palm trees. There aren't many palm trees here. It's just too cold. But they will eat the conifers and the ferns. In doing so, they spread the seeds of those plants. I read an article that says the grasslands have diminished by twenty percent in the five years since dinosaurs were first introduced to the park. This is taking away the grasses and bushes that modern age animals eat. Eventually, if left alone, this whole area will return to a completely dinosaurian habitat. The vegetation and even the geography will be changed by their impact. It will be the only place like it in the world."

"It already is." She nodded to the flock of Hadrosaurs running along the edge of the valley. Caleb swiveled the camera around and focused on the flock. The large creatures rolled like a tide into the Seven Graves River. As they pushed across, Caleb noted the alarm in their eyes. He wondered what had spooked them.

At the same time, the antelope bleated its alert call. Too small to cross the heavy currents of the Seven Graves, they dashed uphill to the safety of the mountain sides.

Simultaneously, the Triceratops bunched together, horns up and frills back. They stamped the ground nervously.

"What's going on?" Sadie asked.

Caleb scanned the valley but didn't see anything. "I don't know. Maybe it's us?" he offered, but that didn't feel right to him. Generally, animals don't run at things that scare them, so the Hadrosaurs running in their direction and off into the river because of Caleb and Sadie's presence didn't make sense.

"My parents have this dog that likes to tuck its tail under its butt and stare at the closet door. It just gets scared. Maybe these dinosaurs do, too."

"Maybe, but just to be safe, why don't we get to higher ground? If we're lucky, there's a small predator out there that we aren't seeing, perhaps a Velociraptor. We might get to see real live raptors hunting Triceratops."

"Wouldn't that be cool?" Sadie said.

As they climbed up the rocks, completely immune to the park's dangers, Sadie asked, "So what's more dangerous, a Velociraptor or a T-Rex?"

They stopped to catch their breath and drink some water. Caleb said, "I wouldn't want either after me. A. T-Rex is the closest thing to a land shark the world will ever get. They're full of teeth, eat just about anything they can shove down their mouth, and have been known to track their prey for tens of miles. But whereas the T-Rex is a solitary predator, Velociraptors are social predators. They are as keen and goal-oriented as wolves. But from what I've heard, while both are popular dinosaurs and what everybody wants to photograph, they aren't the most dangerous dinosaurs here. There is the Allosaurus, which has a voracious appetite, something small called a Coelophysis, which is as small as that Bambiraptor we saw but hunts in packs, and then there is the Majungasaurus, a different apex predator with a shorter snout than a T-Rex, but it's like a cat. That one will just hold its prey by the neck until they asphyxiate. Of course, the prey of a Majungasaurus tends to be sauropods much bigger than us, so I don't know what it'd do to us."

"You've really thought about this a lot," Sadie said with a laugh.

"I've had a lot of time, especially recently."

"Yeah, sorry about your wife. I can't believe she left you."

He waved it off. "I'm no saint, Bucky. You know that better than anyone else."

"You're not that bad."

"I cheated on my wife."

Sadie reached for his hand. "You're still a good guy, Caleb."

"I never told her about that night, you know that? The entire three years we were married, I never mentioned it."

"Why would you? I've never told anyone."

"Nobody?" his eyes searched hers, grasping for something that his life had been missing.

"I'm pretty certain none of us have talked about it." Then she said, "Earlier, I got mad at you, and I shouldn't have. The truth is, you're right. About the tattoos. But if anyone asks, I have other stories for them.

Nobody has ever pieced it together, and they never will. I won't give them enough of the story."

Caleb couldn't resist giving her a once over to look for tattoos. She noticed.

"I'll show you one of the others." She pulled her shirt up over her belly.

Caleb closed his eyes and shook his head. She waited. When he opened them, he saw the scars dripping down from the top of her rib cage around her abdomen and to the back of her rib cage. Green and flowering ivy had been tattooed over the scars. The tattoos reached up under her shirt like gentle fingers reaching for her breasts.

"I'm not going to show you all of it, though," she said.

He clenched his jaw as the memories rushed up from the back of his head. The past still cut just as deep.

She lowered her shirt and put her hand on his shoulder. "It's in the past, Caleb. I'm stronger for it."

"You take it and you take it, and you always come back for more. I couldn't do that. I know you don't feel it, but you're the strongest one of us. Hell, you're the only one who's not a total failure."

"That's not true," she replied.

"Uh, you're an accountant and you drive a BMW."

"You had a wife, and you were a teacher."

"Had. Were. I'm not following you here."

"Julie had a business. She went wingsuiting, for Christ's sake! And Ethan does whatever the hell he wants any time he wants. He's freer than any of us."

Caleb led Sadie back into the trees. "You're living a good life, Bucky."

She wiped sudden tears from her eyes. "I haven't dated anyone in years, Caleb. I haven't even tried. I've never swiped right. And what makes it so sad and sick is that once this guy at work asked me out, and I shut him down. I wouldn't do it. I'm too scared, Caleb. I can't handle that kind of rejection."

"Hey, hey," Caleb said. He enveloped her into his arms and kissed her on the forehead, a human contact that felt so foreign and so welcome at the same time.

"On the way here, this total jerk barista at the coffee bar called my name, and I didn't answer. I guess I was thinking too much about you guys and the trip. So he yelled out, 'Hey, Patches McPatchey Face.' It was stupid, but I didn't say anything. I grabbed my cup and left. I don't fight back. I'm not a fighter."

He pushed her away so that he could look her in the face and said, "You are the strongest person I know. And you are my best family."

"You're mine, too, Caleb. I wish we'd stayed in touch better."

Before he could say more, a large bang cracked in the distance.

5

Ethan and Julie lay low in the grass, their eyes peering through the top strands. The T-Rex stood over the wingsuits they'd shed, sniffing and poking at the clothes.

"We need to call the park service," Julie said, fiddling with the radio.

"Cut that out!" Ethan hissed. He slapped her hand so she couldn't adjust the volume knob.

"They will come get us, Ethan."

"And they'll throw us in jail for the next six to ten years of our lives."

"But at least we'll be alive."

Ethan pinched his nose and tried to center himself. "I want to live, too, but this park covers hundreds of square miles. I doubt there are any Park Rangers close by. If we call them, we are more likely to alert the T-Rex to our presence than we are the rangers, and it would take them hours to get to us. They can't help us yet."

"Okay."

"The problem is this whole valley is downwind of him," Ethan said.

"How do you know it's a him?" Julie asked casually.

"What?"

"I'm just saying. I don't see a giant T-Rex dong hanging out, do you?"

"When would I have seen a T-Rex's junk?"

Julie changed topics. "I've got an idea. Follow me."

Staying low, they crawled on their bellies in a 90-degree angle, scratching their arms and legs along the sharp rocks and stickers.

"Where are we going? The river is that way," Ethan said, pointing back down the valley. "We aren't really any farther from the T-Rex," he said, peering back over his shoulder at the T-Rex, who was ripping their clothes apart. "And *she's* going to get tired of what's left of our wingsuits and come for us."

"I remembered something I saw when we were flying low over the valley. By the way, are these cameras still recording?"

"Yes."

"We're going to get some awesome footage."

They entered a small area of trampled grass. On the far end, not thirty feet away, three armored bodies nosed the rough ground. Two bodies were much smaller than the larger mother.

"Um, Julie. That's a dinosaur," Ethan said.

"An Ankylosaurus, and she will be our savior."

The dinosaur mother noted the two humans and stopped chewing as she considered whether they were something she could ignore or needed to kill.

Julie and Ethan froze.

"Don't look her in the eye," Ethan said out of the side of his face. They both shifted their gaze.

The Ankylosaurus growled. There was a bit of Maria Brink to the dinosaur's growl. Ethan was a fan of the band 'In This Moment' and couldn't help thinking of the singer, Maria Brink, when the dinosaur made its throaty sound.

The mother shuffled to the side. Her babies moved with her like an overly practiced band maneuver. Her tail raised up higher than her head. The spiked tail ended in a giant bone protrusion that looked like it could harness the power of Thor's hammer.

"Oh, that's dangerous," Julie said. They backed away from her as she waved the hammer in the air. Her growl practically sizzled as she glared at them menacingly. The warning was more than enough.

"So this was a bad idea," Ethan said as they backed away.

"It was an idea, though."

A hot wind brushed Julie's hair forward off her shoulders. They jumped to the side as the Tyrannosaurus Rex chomped down on them. If not for an excited flare of nostrils, they would have been dead.

The mother Ankylosaurus hissed angrily at the T-Rex. It sounded like a bow being dragged across a fiddle string the wrong way.

The Tyrannosaurus responded with a bellowing threat. Julie and Ethan ran for cover behind the Ankylosaurus. As Ethan ran, he had to duck to keep from being clobbered by the dinosaur's deadly club. One hit would be enough to shatter every bone in his body.

With an angry mother between her and her prey, Ethan watched the Tyrannosaurus consider its options. She tried going left, then right, but the mother, not realizing the carnivore's true intentions, stayed between the T-Rex and her babies, and hence, Ethan and Julie. She waved her clubbed tail warningly. That hammer colliding with a T-Rex leg may not kill it, but it might break its ankles and render it incapable of hunting, or susceptible to other killers until it healed. The law of the land was movement, and even an apex predator like a T-Rex was dropped down the food chain if it couldn't walk or stand.

While the Tyrannosaurus patiently waited for the tail to swing, Ethan and Julie took advantage of the moment to disappear into the tall grass and flee back to the river.

With one eye on the club, the T-Rex watched the two humans escape. She was curious about these creatures. She had seen and smelled them before, but not ones like these, and they smelled very good. They had escaped from the shell-rock-thing he had destroyed. She had thought it another armored piece of meat, like this one in front of him, but the first one did not move its legs and did not taste good. Parts of it smelled good, but even those parts tasted badly. But then when one of the people ran out of the shell-rock-thing, she had a chance to bite him, and his meat was good and soft in his mouth. He was a new taste, and the Tyrannosaur wanted more of it. Suddenly, more soft-skins ran away, and she knew she wanted to chase them until they got tired and she could eat them, too. They were not fast. But they were crafty.

And now this rock-shell, maybe-prey. It was very big and very dangerous, but it had two smaller, less armored rock-shells beneath it. They were definitely prey. She could eat them and the soft-skins, too. She just needed to pin the rock-shell's head down to the ground.

The club swung at her. It was a warning. She stepped forward cautiously. The Ankylosaurus waited for her to move close enough or give up and walk away. The T-Rex took one more step, testing the mother. She bit on it, swinging long and hard. Her tail swung back and forth in two even strokes, but as soon as the tail swung outward and away from the Tyrannosaurus, she pounced. Her powerful, meaty leg surged forward and slammed down on the Ankylosaurus's neck. The armored beast struck at her with her tail, but now she could easily move out of the way. She wailed. The two babies dug in closer to her. She would take care of them later.

For now, she would take care of this Ankylosaurus bit by bit. Her long maw reached down and snapped at one of her legs, which she was curling underneath her horned sides. The T-Rex hooked one leg in her mouth and pulled it out. Her jaw snapped shut. Fresh, warm blood sputtered into her mouth. Soon, the mother and her babies would be dead, and then she would go after the new meat. The soft-skin-prey.

6

Caleb heard the roar. Moments later, Ethan and Julie appeared, running low to the ground keeping under cover of the high grass.

"What's going on?" he asked Sadie. "Why aren't they in their wingsuits?"

"Over there," she said.

Caleb followed her finger pointed over the valley. About a mile away, a large Tyrannosaurus Rex was stripping the flesh from another dinosaur, an Ankylosaurus by the looks of it.

"They'll be fine as long as the T-Rex is eating."

"And then what?"

Caleb considered this for a moment. "We better get going. I've read that a T-Rex can follow a scent for miles."

They scrambled, shoving their gear back into their packs and running down the trail.

As they hit the slope, they half-collapsed onto the trail and skidded into Ethan and Julie, who were covered in cuts and bruises.

"What happened to you?" Caleb asked.

"We sorta ran into a T-Rex," Julie said.

In the distance, the T-Rex roared. It sounded as deafening and discordant as a Metallica concert.

"It's chasing us," Ethan added. "It has our scent."

"The river," Caleb said. He led them along the edge of the mountain side.

"What are we going to do at the river?" Julie asked.

"We need a boundary between us and the T-Rex. If we have a boundary between us, maybe he'll give up on tracking us. I saw it on a documentary. If we cross the Seven Graves, maybe it will leave us alone."

"And if it doesn't?" Julie asked.

"Hope it doesn't swim."

The herd of Triceratops watched them warily. Their frills had changed colors dramatically from a dull green to bright red as blood pumped through their arteries. It was a defense mechanism meant to distract predators and focus them on attacking their armor. As Caleb glanced over, they glared at him. He wondered how much it would take for one of the dinosaurs to attack. He didn't want to find out.

One of the Triceratops stomped his clawed foot on the ground, throwing a cloud of dust into the air.

"Everybody slow down," Caleb warned.

"I don't want to slow down. There's a T-Rex back there," Julie said. "She wanted to eat me."

In his best even-keel voice, Caleb said, "And there's a whole herd of Triceratops ready to charge us if we don't calm down. Remember, no dinosaur is used to seeing people."

"I think we should listen to Caleb," Sadie said, taking Julie by the arm and slowing her down.

"Easy for you guys to say," Ethan said. "But I'm telling you, when that T-Rex decides to charge, nothing is standing in her way. We had to get behind an Ankylosaurus to slow her down." He chose his pronouns carefully. "The T-Rex killed the other dinosaurs, and from the sound of it, she's back on us. And trust me when I say this, guys, that Triceratops may be really big but it's also super fast."

One of the Triceratops bleated angrily at the group. He shook his head back and forth, a universal sign to back the eff off. Caleb spread his arms wide around the group and pushed them away. They backed up the slope away from the Triceratops.

The Triceratops decided they weren't backing away fast enough, and he charged into the group, tossing his horns side to side. Everybody screamed and scattered. The ground thundered under the massive weight of the Triceratops. The Triceratops concentrated on Julie in particular. As she jumped to one side, he followed her, lowering his horns.

Julie was lucky in that she was too short to be impaled on one of the horns of the Triceratops. And she was twice lucky because she didn't fall down. If she had lost her footing on the slope, the Triceratops would have smashed her face into the packed earth. Instead, he nipped her calf. She jumped in shock, and that's when the dinosaur used the horns it was famous for to scoop her body up and fling her ten feet to the side. She crashed into a rock outcropping and fell limp.

"Julie!" the others yelled.

The Triceratops turned his attention on Ethan. Ethan wasn't faster than the Triceratops, but he could jump a lot higher. He bolted to the top of a nearby boulder. The Triceratops exploded into the rock with enough power to knock Ethan off of the top, but Ethan put one foot on top of a horn and hopped back to safety.

The Triceratops raised up on his hind legs and slammed down on the rock. Ethan ducked behind the blocky stone. His heart was beating like a woodpecker in his chest.

"Over here!" Caleb yelled, waving his arms at the dinosaur.

The Triceratops snorted and did an about-face. Ethan peered around the rock and saw that Caleb was alone and exposed. He also wasn't nearly as nimble as Ethan. So he pulled out the big noise maker gun and fired it at the Triceratops. The deafening sound was like a thunderclap from twenty feet away.

The Triceratops bleated an alarm and ran away. The herd followed.

Caleb, Ethan, and Sadie ran to Julie, who was still laying where she'd fallen.

"Don't be dead," Sadie cried.

Caleb turned Julie over. He leaned down and listened to her chest and her mouth. "She's alive, but she's unconscious."

"We need a stretcher," Sadie said.

"Jackets and hiking poles," Ethan said.

Caleb had no idea what he was talking about, but he stripped off his backpack anyway. Wilderness survival was Ethan's bailiwick, not his. "Jacket's in the back pocket."

Ethan unzipped the pack and found the rain jacket. He pulled the sleeves inside-out, then did the same to the purple jacket Sadie produced. He extended the hiking poles and shoved them up the sleeves and out the sleeve holes to create an improvised stretcher.

"I never would have thought of that," Caleb said. "Cool."

Caleb and Ethan lifted Julie onto the stretcher. Julie grunted and reached for her side. Her eyes fluttered awake.

"My side!" she said in sudden alarm.

"I think maybe you cracked a rib," Caleb said, having felt along her rib cage while Ethan constructed the stretcher. "Does anything else hurt? What about your back?"

She shook her head and grumbled, "I don't think so."

"Rest, then. We're getting you out of here."

"The radio," she groaned.

Caleb noticed the radio for the first time.

Ethan said, "You got it, Playa."

"Soon as we get you across the river," Caleb said.

Ethan led the stretcher toward the banks of the Seven Graves. "We've got a problem," he said. "This is a pretty swift river."

"Can you walk her across it?"

"Not easily."

A giant sweat ring radiated outward from Ethan's neck and ran down his shirt. He could feel the adrenaline crashing. "We need to get somewhere fast. I don't know how much more energy I have left in me." He scanned down the river, hoping for an easier crossing.

"Upriver." The section of the river had a small fall, less than five feet high, overlooking the deeper water. Large, wet rocks jutted from the shallow water.

Julie groaned as they walked up along the Seven Graves. Sadie collected some of her Advil and gave it to Julie to swallow with some water.

"Thanks, Bucky," she said.

The T-Rex made a noise that resonated over the sound of the rushing water.

"That's a lot closer," Ethan said. He edged out into the river. Eons ago, a giant limestone slab had fallen next to the fall. Algae turned the flat rock green and slick. Cautiously, he settled his first boot down into the water. He shivered. The Seven Graves felt icy cold as it sluiced down into his boots.

"Ouch," Julie called out. "Careful."

"Sorry, Playa."

He moved his next foot into the water, concentrating on keeping his balance and not losing his footing.

"Careful," he shouted back to Caleb. "This rock is slick." Just as he said it, he slipped on the rock. He quickly corrected himself.

Sadie glanced back across the valley. "She's coming," she said. "You've got to move faster!"

Ethan shouted to Caleb, "On my time. Left foot, right foot, left foot, right foot." He pointed to make sure there was no confusion about what "right" and "left" meant. With each step, they moved father out onto the limestone.

"Hurry," Sadie said, patting Caleb on the back.

"I'm going as fast as I can. If we slip, we lose Julie."

"If you don't hurry, you'll lose us all."

Caleb glanced over his shoulder. The T-Rex was rampaging across the valley, her nose pointed like a torpedo directly at them.

"Faster!" he shouted to Ethan. "Left, right, left, right!" he said at a much quicker pace. Up ahead, Ethan tried to keep up.

Suddenly, Caleb's foot slipped out behind him, and he fell WHAM right on his knee. He howled in pain. He also made sure not to lose Julie, who had to grab the poles painfully to keep from flopping overboard.

Julie opened her eyes. An upside-down T-Rex was running at her. She screamed at the top of her lungs. Sadie screamed reflexively.

The T-Rex made a sound like the low thrum of a rhythm guitarist.

Caleb pushed up. Blood trailed from his knee into the river and over the waterfall's edge. Ethan began to run, and Caleb ran after him, all pretense for being careful gone.

Sadie pushed Caleb forward, her hand always on his back.

Ethan fell down again, this time on his butt. As Ethan fell, Caleb slid, too. It was like a domino effect. Suddenly they were all covered up to their belly buttons in river water that was fed from mountain springs.

The T-Rex hopped into the river bank, her tail wiggling playfully behind him. Her belly was full of Ankylosaurus. Now she was mainly curious about the smells coming from these creatures. She did not know about the smells of accounting offices and high schools and bars. The smell of the chemicals in Julie's hair was new to her, too. She wanted to explore these smells and soft tissues. She just had to decide which one first. Fortunately, the soft-skins decided for her.

Ethan tried to stand back up. The T-Rex snapped down at him. Ethan leapt at the last second, his body flailing over the side of the waterfall.

As Ethan fell, the others jumped, too. Caleb held on to Julie as he plunged into the water. The stretcher snapped on one of the rocks, and then she floated up, gasping painfully for air.

Caleb grabbed hold of her and pulled her close to him as he kicked away. The Tyrannosaur's giant head plunged into the river water, which was at least five feet deep under the waterfall. The T-Rex came up with nothing. She studied them with keen interest, deciding which to choose next in her game of "bobbing for humans."

Thankfully, the current pulled Caleb and Julie away from the waterfall. Julie moaned in Caleb's ear. She was making a small sound, and he knew it was because the pain of using her lungs was more than she could handle at the moment.

From his left, Sadie swam to him. She was doing her best to keep afloat, but something in her pack was weighing her down.

"Drop the pack," Caleb said.

"No." She forced herself above water. He reached out a hand to her. She grabbed it, and he pulled her close.

"We have to stay in the middle where the current is swiftest.

She didn't say anything.

"Where's Ethan?"

He followed her eyes. Behind them, the Tyrannosaur's head dove once more. It came back up, dragging Ethan out of the surge. His skin was pale. *How long was he under?* Caleb wondered.

Suddenly, the adventurer sprang to life. He reached for the T-Rex and stabbed her gums with a pocket knife. The predator let go, and Ethan fell back into the water. He came up ten feet farther down the river, but still out of reach from the group. His head was face up, but he wasn't moving.

The T-Rex walked, then slipped on the limestone and stumbled down the waterfall. She landed with a crash in the lower section of the river. Her fall caused a wave to push the four even farther down the river. Slowly, the T-Rex climbed out of the Seven Graves and began to walk along the river shore, but by then, the four were far gone. The swift river current had taken them around three bends and dumped them twice into surging white water.

She belted out a sharp, sad bark. Her play had disappeared.

Exhausted and half-drowned, the gang bobbed in the water as they continued travelling at the mercy of the Seven Graves. They clung to each other desperately.

PART 2: PREDATOR PREY ROLES

BANION'S MISTAKE

Greedy eyes watched the herd of bison cross the rolling hills and enter the grasslands. This late in summer, the dying grass had transformed from green stalks to dry kindling drained of nutritional value. The herd was ever on the move, searching for better sustenance. A male rolled in the dirt while the females watched over their spring calves.

Hours ago, the Velociraptors had chosen this spot for their ideal trap. The smell of bison was heavy on the dirt; the bison would return daily. The raptors climbed up the bark of the spruce and lodgepole pines at the edge of the grasslands. Their claws were ideal for finding crevices and perches from which they could attack. Once in position, they waited patiently for the bison to come.

By mid-day, the sun began pushing waves of heat too intense for the bison's comfort levels. The shade of the trees beckoned to them, and the ungulates followed. It was part of their daily migration from feeding place to feeding place, picking up sustenance wherever they could find it.

First, several females entered the woods. They stood under the shade unchallenged. Summer made predators like wolves and mountain lions desperate if food sources dwindled, but the herd had encountered fewer predators this year than most. And if a wolf or mountain lion did jump out at him, these forward scouts would either return to the herd or gore the predator themselves.

But nothing happened that afternoon.

They stood there, a symbol of American strength and freedom, rays of sunlight cutting through the trees.

An odd scent lingered on the ground, but the bison did not know what it was. It was something they had never smelled before. The smell came from the trees and then disappeared, and without any further evidence to support what this strange smell belonged to, the bison licked their noses clean and ignored it.

They trudged deeper into the woods. The herd followed. There were ten females, an older male, and four calves in the harem. The reddish calves were not yet weaned from their mothers.

The herd moved into the cool shade. Here and there, they discovered spots where the grass was more tender and lovely than they found earlier in the day. They grinded the grass in their teeth with the contented attention span of the largest land animal in North America.

Without a signal and in unison, the Velociraptors seemed to select the female and calf to slaughter. Quietly, they drifted down the trees like spiders on silk, guided by their lust for body juices and flesh.

Three raptors landed on top of the female, who was completely taken by surprise. She bleated out her shock as she charged deeper into the trees and back to the herd.

Because of her alarm, the harem pulled together and rolled into a phalanx of horns and brute strength. The calves stayed protected inside the circle. They could hear the alarm of the other bison, but they could not see this new danger.

The female bucked and kicked with enough power to seriously maim a grizzly bear if she hit him the right way. The problem was that these new predators were much smaller than a grizzly. They were barely larger than a wolf. If she could get a hoof in them, they would let go. The problem was they were all on top of her back. She couldn't touch them.

The Velociraptors used their wicked hooks to rend the female's flesh. Their teeth sank into her hump and her back, scraping against her spine.

The unlucky bison rolled onto the ground, hoping to crush the dinosaurs. This tactic had worked with wolves and lions. The bison believed it would work on these strange creatures, too.

The raptors were accustomed to challenging much larger prey. They leaped off the bison and scattered. The bison seized the opportunity and charged the nearest one, positioning her head low to the ground and running as fast as her lungs would allow. This new thing would pay for the pain it had given.

But this creature was faster than a wolf. It easily outran her and scrambled up a tree. From a safe distance, it hissed at her.

And then the other two raptors jumped back on her. Again she charged, but this time she ran back to the herd, blood flying off her like waves of crimson fire.

The herd tried to disperse, but was not quick enough. The female with the two raptors on her back galumphed into the center of the herd.

Surrounded by little fleshlings, the raptors smiled gleefully. But the mother, sensing her mistake, swung wide and exited the phalanx. She tried rolling on them, and again they retreated up the trees. In the meantime, she'd lost a lot of blood, and she didn't have the energy to chase these deviant monsters. She backed up against a tree and prepared to fight them to her dying breath.

Recognizing that the mother wasn't charging because she'd lost too much blood, the raptors slowly returned to the ground, screeching like heavy metal banshees.

Less than thirty yards from her, her calf pleaded to his mama for protection. He was alone and scared.

The third raptor was sneaking up quietly behind the calf. The talons on his front claws were fully open as he approached the calf from behind.

Mother was not having any of that. Ignoring all rules of survival, the mother bison stomped after the raptor. She gave him no warning. Her thundering hooves must have been drowned out by the thundering of his heart and the anticipation of the kill. She put her horn into him and tossed him up in the air.

The dinosaur took the brunt of her charge and was thrown head over heels into the air. He landed with a crash on his back and yelped. The mother reversed course and charged him again. He barely got to his feet by the time she reached him. She rolled like a tide right over him, crushing and stomping him under her hooves. His bones cracked and his insides squished out of his orifices.

When she finished pulverizing the strange, new animal with all the teeth and claws, her hooves were covered in blood, but her nose was dripping with her own blood, too. She felt a weariness in her bones colder than the harshest winters. She turned her head to the other two raptors. They glared hungrily at her from the trees.

Her calf approached her. She walked back to the protection of the herd and stumbled. She had lost too much blood. The adrenaline was wearing off, and all that pain was seeping into her. During the attack, entire strips of her flesh had been peeled off like layers of an onion, revealing bloody muscle beneath.

The herd ate for a bit.

The raptors waited.

In the sky, ravens approached, smelling dead things in the wind.

When the herd finally moved on, a lone female lay alone in the dark, too tired to stand. They had stayed as long as they could. For the good of the herd, they had to return to a warmer location to bed down for the night. It may have been summer, but at this altitude, night time temperatures lowered into the 40s, and they had the calves to think about.

The mother snorted weakly yet defiantly.

The Velociraptors descended from the trees…

7

Caleb, Julie, and Sadie floated for half an hour down the river before they were able to make it back to shore. They huddled together, arms intertwined like locked coils, their heads above water. Caleb would have thought of balls of fire ants floating down a flooded river if not for the fact that he was confused and scared out of his wits. As the evening waned, more creatures came to the river to feed, and they rarely saw anything that didn't want to eat them. Some dinosaurs groaned at them from their hiding places in the foliage. Others appeared. Heads with grinding teeth and angry eyes.

The dinosaurs had frills and horns and crests over their eyes or on top of their heads. And with every call, the dinosaurs seemed to be crying out in unison, "Go away! You do not belong here!"

Caleb could not agree more. He had never felt so unwanted. When he left the school, when he was fired, he had been one of the teachers kids liked. He wasn't "Teacher of the Year" by any stretch, but he had an enthusiasm for science that the kids picked up on.

If he hadn't thrown that punch in the hallway, things might be different. If Jacob Peerson hadn't videotaped it and uploaded it to his YouTube channel, Caleb would still be working there. Principal Matthews, who was still the principal at West Lake High, had told him as much. "You were a good kid when you were here, and you were an even better teacher. But this isn't the 70s and we don't paddle kids. Corporal punishment is forbidden. But for this to have gotten out. Caleb, I can't protect you. I have to let you go. I hope you understand."

They had lost Ethan in one set of rapids. He was barely conscious as it was. Caleb and Sadie called for him. They only stopped when they heard the unmistakable call of the T-Rex.

"How far away do you think she is?"

"I don't know," Caleb answered.

"Is she coming after us?"

"Yes."

Sadie began crying then. He had only seen her cry twice in his life. The first time was horrifying. This second time was heartbreaking.

Ethan woke up face down along the shore of the Seven Graves River. His leg throbbed with pain. He pulled himself up out of the cold water. He rolled his pants up to his knee, exposing a swollen and bruised calf. Three large holes marked where the T-Rex had grabbed him, two on the back of his calf and one on the shin. Ethan gasped. He remembered very little after the T-Rex pulled him up off the waterfall. He remembered the bottom of the falls about twenty feet below him. Didn't he pull his knife? Didn't he fall?

And now he was here. Where was here? *Doesn't matter*, he thought. The first priority in any wilderness survival situation was safety and health. He was injured, but how badly?

His fingers poked and prodded his wounds. Fresh blood oozed out. Ethan winced as fresh spider webs of pain ran up his leg.

He pushed against the sides of his leg where he was bruised the most and groaned. It wasn't an open fracture, but it was swollen like a grapefruit and ugly as hell. His best guess was that a piece of his tibia or fibular was cracked. He thought back to his wilderness first aid training. It was a three-day seminar down in Joshua Tree, but he'd paid close attention and took notes because he believed the information could provide the difference between life and death.

A splint. He'd need a splint. After he drank greedily from the river, he crawled along the banks on his hands and knees searching for a sturdy stick. He found one caught in the high grass. He reached for his knife, then remembered that he lost it in the water, so he ripped his shirt into strips and used those strips to tether his fractured leg to the stick. The stick was longer than his calf and kind of dug into his upper leg, but he didn't have a way of removing the stick, so he left it as-is. He then slowly pulled himself up off the ground, using a nearby tree to get upright.

Pain shot like lightning through his leg. He fell over and stayed down in the mud. He lay like that for ten minutes, and considered staying for ten more, but then he heard the T-Rex. She sounded like she had a lawnmower caught in her throat.

He needed to get going. With any hope, the others swam upstream to the falls. That's what he would have done. The eponymous Dinosaur Falls was where all the tourists watched dinosaurs from the safety of mountain resorts on the other side. With any luck, they could be in a jail cell by morning, and at this point, he'd take a jail cell over being devoured by dinosaurs.

He'd been in jail cells before. It came with the territory when you BASEjumped from places they didn't want you to jump from. But those were God's creations, just like this whole park. So why were they trying to stop him from accessing this property and doing what he wanted? As long as he wasn't destroying the environment or leaving a mess, why should the government dictate to him how long he could stay in a park or that he couldn't jump from its mountain peaks? Sure, rescuers would be needed if he hurt himself, but he was BASEjumping. He wouldn't simply hurt himself. Either he survived or he was human pulp. Those were the two options. And if he was the latter, nobody needed to come after him. He was fine with the idea of his body decomposing by itself in a park somewhere.

But he'd survived before, and he'd survive this one. With a little help, his friends would survive it, too. He felt anxious for them. While they'd all been avid outdoorsmen, Julie was the only other true expert in the group. Caleb had always taken more of a scientific approach to the outdoors. He was less concerned with survival tactics than he was the mating rituals of prairie chickens or whatever.

And Sadie? Sadie, he loved. They all loved her, but she was the last person to save herself, or anyone.

He would meet them at Dinosaur Falls.

Caleb and Sadie swam out of the current and into an eddy. They helped Julie out of the Seven Graves River. She groaned as they stepped out.

Julie leaned against a tree, wincing in pain.

"Do you still have the radio?" Sadie asked.

Julie shook her head despondently.

They were thoroughly soaked, and they were covered in cuts and bruises from bouncing off river rocks. Caleb had tried to use his backpack to cushion them from the blows, but it couldn't prevent all their injuries. They were lucky to escape the river's fury without more serious ailments.

As Sadie walked through the knee-high water to shore, Caleb saw where her wet shorts had ridden up on her and stuck to her hips. White and pink splotches ran down her leg. The tattoo caught his attention. He knew what it represented, the grim reaper waving its sickle over a campfire.

Sadie pulled her shorts down.

"What happened to Ethan?" she asked.

"I lost him," Caleb said.

"We have to go find him," Julie said.

"The falls can't be an hour's hike from here. We could get help there. People could come search for him," Caleb said.

"No," Julie said. "This isn't some random person. This is Ethan. We're not leaving without him."

"We have to go look for him," Sadie said.

"You're right," Caleb admitted. The falls may be close, but this was Ethan. He was like a brother to Caleb, and he needed to find him.

They limped along the edges of the river bank, water sluicing off there wet bodies as they searched the shores and the roots and rocks for any sign of Ethan.

Sadie called out, "Ethan!"

Julie quickly admonished her. "What are you trying to do, call every predator to us?"

"How will he know we're here if we don't call out for him?"

"He'll just have to know."

Caleb didn't like that idea, but he had to admit, it was pragmatic. They'd seen a lot of mean faces peering out at them from the forest when they fled down the river.

Caleb remembered the first time he met Ethan, back in sixth grade going into middle school. "He was the same grade as me," he told the others. "I was just a scared little nerdy kid in a really big world. I liked dinosaurs and 'Dungeons and Dragons' and all these geeky things that made me an easy target. I wore a *Texas-saurus Rex* t-shirt with a T-Rex dressed up like Clint Eastwood. I was clueless. What was funny a year ago was made fun of when I walked down the halls. I felt as low as dirt. And then there was Ethan, dressed in his hiking boots and his bracelets. I swear, he was born with hiking boots. He asked me if I was new to this school, which, yeah, of course I was. He said he was, too. He asked me if I liked dinosaurs. I didn't want to answer, so he said it was okay, he wanted to be an explorer when he grew up, and paleontology was kind of like exploring. It was exploring the past. Immediately I felt better. We've been friends ever since."

Sadie pushed back a stand of brush and reeds. She was relieved to not find his body. "He called me Bucky," she said. "After everything that happened, you know, at Homecoming, he found me in the library working on this science project. He didn't understand it. *What's with those cool soccer balls?* He asked me. I told them they were buckminsterfullerenes. "Bucky balls" for short. *Yo, Bu-cky!* He shouted. After that it was Bucky. I really liked that one."

Julie smiled. "He always found the best in us. I think it made up for his home life. His parents never approved that he was bi-sexual."

"I wasn't there when it happened," Sadie said as they moved down the Seven Graves.

"It was bad. Tenth grade, and people spray-painted all kinds of garbage on his locker. Really hateful words. I was so mad. He told *me* to calm down. *They're just jealous because I get twice the action with women that they do,* he said."

"Most people outside of us thought of him as 'the lover' because he was so open about his sexuality. They were wrong, though," Caleb said. "He wasn't the lover. He was the fighter."

Ethan pulled himself up the side of the tree, then gently placed his foot down on the ground. He winced, but he was able to put pressure on it. The trick was to keep pressure on the inside step rather than the outside. He took one awkward step, stopped to grunt, then took another. With each step, his confidence grew. He walked around several trees, then shuddered.

When he first woke, he thought he'd heard the familiar sound of water crashing against rocks. His instincts were correct. The Seven Graves lowered in elevation thirty feet over the next twenty yards. In front of him lay an obstacle course of slick rocks and mud, all on an incline.

He needed a crutch or a walking stick. The shore offered nothing useful, and the only sticks among the rocks were short and shattered pieces of wood. Perhaps inland he would find something useful. Until then, he'd have to make do.

He maneuvered down the incline with the grace and power of an eighty year old woman with a hip replacement.

The first time he slipped, he felt it in his tailbone. When he went down, his butt hit the edge of a large stone.

Standing was even harder. He had no tree to use to lift himself up. He shuffled on his butt down the side of the rocks till he came to a two-foot drop-off, perfect for getting himself back upright. He inched his feet down into the soft mud and stood up. Standing felt good. He was halfway down the incline. The sound of the river against the rocks was actually very relaxing. He knew people who used sound apps to help them get to sleep. He always wondered why anyone would choose an app over the real thing. Just get out there and find a river to sleep next to, right?

Something slammed into his back. He fell face forward down onto an algae-covered rock. Between the smooth algae and his momentum, he shot down along the rock face and slid ten more feet, crashing foot-first into a boulder before dropping into a pool of mud. Ethan hollered as he bounced off the boulder. A lightning crash of unequivocal pain, followed by the sound of a stick snapping in two, heralded the complete disintegration of his splint.

Sweating, Ethan pushed his head up out of the mud and looked around. What hit him?

Something chirped from up along the rock face. It had black feathers and sharp little teeth.

"You," Ethan growled. "I should have killed you when I had the chance."

The Bambiraptor hissed.

Ethan yelled loudly and flung a heap of mud at the raptor. It watched the mud ball sail wide and splatter against the rocks.

"Go away!" Ethan yelled.

The Bambiraptor cocked his head to the side.

"That's right. You heard me, Bambi. Get your ass out of here before I kick it."

The raptor skipped down the rocks. Ethan searched the mud for a rock or anything he could use as a weapon, but his fingers found nothing but mud.

With weapons out of the question, he tried a different tactic. While there were no guidelines for dinosaur encounters, he knew that standing tall would often deter most non-extinct predators. So he gathered up all the courage he could muster and forced himself to stand. He screamed at the bottom of his lungs. It was something primal and guttural, a sound he'd never made before. Reluctantly, his broken leg accepted the weight of his body, and Ethan stood upright.

The raptor licked its lips. A row of sharp and shiny teeth reflected in the sunlight.

Suddenly, Ethan smelled something sweet in the air. Candy. Specifically, M&Ms. He'd always loved M&Ms growing up. They were his treat every day walking home from school as a kid. He would stop at the convenience store and buy a packet of M&Ms. Sometimes the mini's, and he'd go with Peanut M&Ms, too, but his real pleasure was always the black wrapper. The original M&Ms.

He ate so many, his car in high school was littered with discarded wrappers. So the first time he'd had sex was in the back seat of his car (Skyler), the smell of the wrappers was mixed with the smell of their sex. Skyler was amazing.

Skyler's older brothers didn't think so much about him. They were the ones who spray-painted "slut" and "whore" and worse things on his locker at school. He never lived that down.

But that wasn't where the smell directed him. He remembered another time he was covered in mud. He remembered the fear that was palpable in the air. Spilled M&Ms. Lyme. Blood. Pine.

He'd been knocked down in the mud and called names. He was bleeding from the side. He lifted his head up from the ground and yelled.

He'd stood up then, and he'd stand up now.

"Come on! Show me what you've got!"

The raptor hopped down at the edge of the mud and considered him. He thought he made a big enough target. His arms and legs were out wide. He yelled again. Yelling was all he had. He didn't dare take a step toward the dinosaur.

The raptor feinted.

Ethan took a step back before he realized what he was doing. Gargantuan amounts of pain lanced up and down his leg. The pain made his leg collapse, and he fell down in the mud.

The little dinosaur jumped on him. Ribbons of pain cut along his back. He rolled to his side as the raptor jumped off him.

"Argh!" He wouldn't give up. That was the difference between those who died and those who survived. The ones who lived never gave up. He shoved one hand in the ground behind him and willed his body out of the mud pool.

The little dinosaur sat at the edge of the pool and watched Ethan drag himself out.

A ragged red line traced his passage back into the mud pool. The dinosaur took three light steps into the pool and licked at his blood.

"You leave that alone! That's my blood!" In his ears, he could hear his threat diminished. He was weakening. Had night set? Everything seemed darker.

"The joke's on you, Bambi. I've been eating nothing but sugar for twenty years. You'll probably get diabetes eating me."

Finally, Ethan reached solid ground. His hands dug into the hard earth. All he needed was a rock, a tree branch, anything to improvise as a weapon.

As his hands searched for a weapon, the raptor dragged him back.

He kicked at it with his boot. A lucky hit, the heel of his boot connected with the small dinosaur's head. It yelped in pain and ran away.

"That's right, little dino. I can do this all day. ALL DAY!"

But from the back of his mind came the counter argument: *No, you cannot. You're running out of energy and blood. You cannot keep fighting.*

As if to prove his point, the raptor was back. It tugged at his leg.

"Let go," Ethan mumbled. In his mind, he kicked at the raptor again. He wasn't sure if he actually kicked at the raptor or not, though.

The raptor's head ducked down. Pain erupted from his calf. When the Bambiraptor's head appeared again, it was covered in his blood. He could swear it smiled at him.

From out of the trees, three more raptors appeared. They jumped from rock to rock and danced around Ethan. And they weren't planning to drag him back into the pit. They wanted to eat him where he lay.

He took a defensive position, swinging his arms and legs at the raptors dipping their sharp teeth into his body. They bit his forearms and his shin bones. He kept swinging. They kept ducking out of the way like a well-trained prize fighter. And he felt so drained and weighted down. Moving his arms was like moving slabs of concrete.

When he could fight no more, he dropped his arms at his side and inhaled sharply. The raptors took the opportunity to bite into his soft belly.

Oh, gee, it's up to my knee, he thought.

"I hope you choke on my bones!" he growled defiantly.

And then he was flying again. He was soaring over mountains that he'd hiked and packed. He was diving in his wing suit, diving like a cliff swallow along the sides of mountains. Nobody could stop him here, and nobody could catch him. All they could do was wave at him from the ground.

There was something else going on. In the woods where nobody could be seen. There was a darkness in the woods, a darkness that he avoided. The woods were a good place, a place where he could be free. But not these woods. Dark, insidious things lurked in the shadows of those trees. Death lived there.

A moment lived there. One dark, abysmal moment. The nadir of his existence.

Many moments had happened since that one dark moment, but he wondered if he'd ever really escaped its coils. In all his jumps, he'd always been jumping to something. But maybe he was jumping away from something. It was a leap he'd never truly made because the kind of thing that happened in those woods never really leaves the soul.

"Run, Sadie," Ethan said in the last moment of his life.

8

"He was so full of it," Caleb said. "He dated maybe six people in high school, freshman to...." Caleb stopped as he rounded a large pine.

"What is it?" Julie asked.

"Don't come over here," Caleb said. His head was swimming. He reached out for a tree to balance himself.

"What?"

"No!" Caleb pushed her away from the bushes. "Don't go over there!" His face strained. He gritted his teeth. He sucked in a breath. Anything to keep the tears at bay. They came anyway. Fat droplets that plopped from his eyes on the ground.

Sadie stood paralyzed. She hadn't seen what was in the bushes, and she didn't want to ask.

"I have to see."

"No, Julie. You can't unsee that."

"Unsee what?" Sadie had to ask. It was like it hadn't happened until it was vocalized.

"Ethan's dead."

Julie fell down crying and spasming in pain at the same time. Her chest told her not to sob, but her body was reacting instinctively. Caleb held her gently in his arms. Sadie watched them both as she snuck around Caleb and looked into the mud pool. She gasped.

There wasn't much of him left. But his helmet was there, and so was his head. The nose and eyes and lips had been pulled off. His arms and legs were gone, as were most of his insides. Clean, white bones lay on the blood-soaked ground.

If not for the scraps of cloth and the helmet, she wasn't sure there was enough of him left to be identified.

9

Dinosaur Falls was the main geological feature of the national park. A wide, concave-shaped drop at the end of the Seven Graves River, the falls plummeted fifty feet into Banion's Mistake, a crystal clear lake full of rainbow trout and other native fish species. The lake itself was so mesmerizing as to be the subject of many photographers. Ancient glaciers had ground the boulders into small stones so brightly colored some people nicknamed Banion's Mistake "Skittle Lake." The colorful lake rivaled the beautiful colors of Emerald Lake in British Columbia, or even Lake McDonald and Avalanche Lake in Glacier National Park.

Of course, as tantalizing as the natural beauty was, nobody visited Dinosaur Falls for the actual falls. They wanted to see the dinosaurs that frequented Banion's Mistake. The cool waters and lush vegetation attracted gargantuan sauropods, herds of duck-billed dinosaurs, and the Triceratops. With all those giant herbivores at the pool, Banion's Mistake was known for also bringing in the large meat eaters: the T-Rexes, the Allosaurus, and the Carnotaurus.

Twenty meters from the far end of the lake stood giant, electrified fences and concrete blocks to keep the dinosaurs inside the national park. From the safety of cabins, hotel balconies, and visitor center observation decks, people could watch the dinosaurs interact. For those who couldn't make the journey to Dinosaur Falls National Park, cameras were attached to the tops of the fence posts. They swayed back and forth across the lake, broadcasting every dinosaurian movement on a dedicated YouTube channel.

This late at night, though, nobody was out. It was too dark to see any dinosaurs who might be there, and most of the larger ones preferred to interact during the morning and evening hours. The tourists and rangers had returned to the safety of their dinosaur-themed buildings. When Julie, Caleb, and Sadie arrived, nobody was there to see them.

And the cameras' default setting focused the lenses on the falls and the lake.

"Hey!" Sadie yelled.

"It's no use," Julie wheezed. "They can't hear or see you."

"The good news is, we just have to survive the night, and we should be rescued," Caleb said.

"And the bad news," Julie whispered, "is that the T-Rex will catch up to us way before sunrise hits."

Back at Ethan's body, Julie had wanted to fall down and give up. Her business was in ruin, she was bankrupt, and her friend and one-time lover was dead. Caleb mourned the loss of his brother. Sadie cried for the man she'd always looked up to. Their grieving was interrupted by the grinding sound of the T-Rex, reminding them that she was on her way to them and had not given up on their trail. They could mourn and die, or they could run.

They ran.

Even Julie, with her ribs on fire, ran.

They arrived at the falls broken, bleeding, and hungry. Caleb searched his pack for anything edible. He found a bag of trail nuts that wasn't soggy, but also some Granola bars that hung limply in his hands.

He took a handful of the nuts and handed the bag to Sadie and Julie. They devoured it in seconds.

"What do we do?" Sadie asked.

"Well, the way I see it, in about three hours a T-Rex is going to come bursting out of that tree line and charge us."

"Should we keep running?"

"This is the best place to be seen."

"But we're trapped."

"So is he," Julie said.

"What do you mean?" Caleb asked.

Weakly, she nodded over the edge of the waterfall. "That fall would kill him."

"How do we get him over?" Sadie asked.

They stood at the edge of the falls and pondered this for a few minutes.

"What if we don't try to lure him over?" Caleb said.

"That'd make us dino-munchies," Sadie said. "I'd rather not be that."

"I'm thinking of something else," Caleb said. He surveyed the falls, then dropped his pack and started rummaging through it. He pulled out a small wood axe.

"You're going to kill a T-Rex with an axe?" Sadie asked, not amused.

"No, I'm going to incapacitate it. I've read that Tyrannosaurs are so big, that falling down can injure them. I've also read about how their ankles are their weak spot."

Julie said with sudden realization, "The Ankylosaurus. It was sweeping for the T-Rex's ankles back in the valley."

"There you go," Caleb said. "I think one good chop will be enough to take out its Achilles. We do that, and the T-Rex won't be able to chase us."

"Great idea, but one problem," Sadie said, her voice trembling. "How do you get behind a T-Rex's ankle?"

"Bait," Julie said.

10

Caleb's pack had some ibuprofen pills. Julie took all of them. The pain was getting worse. The adrenaline rush of going over the falls and being swept down-river, then finding Ethan…it was all coming to a head. Her body was reacting to the lack of adrenaline. Pain was erupting along her ribs. The ibuprofen would help a little, but not enough. She needed to be coherent. She needed to be strong for Caleb and Sadie. Neither one of them were as strong in the outdoors as she and Ethan. Case in point, Caleb and Sadie were standing in the middle of the falls, sharpening sticks and wedging them between rocks as some sort of trap for the T-Rex. They were tired and panicked. She was in pain, but she was calm.

"Stay calm," she said as loud as she could. "Don't panic. That is the secret to any survival situation. Go to the internet, go to Backpacker magazine, take a course on wilderness EMS, they all start with the same premise: don't overreact to a situation. Keep your composure and stay level-headed."

Julie dug around in the dirt, picking up pine needles and old leaves.

"I feel like that's one of those things that people say or write, but once you're being hunted by the world's largest carnivore, everything gets thrown out the window," Sadie said.

"That's giving in to the fear. You can't give in to it. If you do, your body will burn up its resources, and you'll make mistakes. Those sticks aren't wedged in deep enough." She pointed to a few sticks that Caleb had just finished placing in the falls. They had detached from the ground and were floating away.

"If you're going to do that right, think like a beaver," Julie said. "You need big rocks behind the sticks, and little rocks and mud in front. Otherwise, the current is going to take it all away."

While they scrambled to repair the trap, Julie clumsily dropped all the tinder in a pile next to her kindling sticks. These were all collected next to two larger logs that she didn't have to move. In her condition, she wasn't ready to move logs around.

After she assembled the fire, she lit the tinder. She gave it a little breath, and then her fire began to blaze.

Caleb and Sadie came over. They were soaked from being in the river.

"Hey, won't that attract the T-Rex?" Caleb asked.

"Fire is bright, and a campfire is undeniably human." She pointed to the hotels and cabins a little over a mile away from them. "This fire may save us quicker than anything else if they see it."

"We need something else," she said. She opened up Caleb's pack.

"Let me help you," he said. "What do you need?"

"Your sterno and a shirt." He handed her an old shirt from the San Francisco Museum. The shirt featured the bones of a T-Rex.

"There was a time people could only guess at what a T-Rex looked like, or how it behaved," he said. "I was going to take a photo with this shirt in the foreground and dinosaurs in the back."

"That would've looked really cool on Instagram," Sadie said.

"Don't give up on your Instagram dreams, Moose," Julie said. "You may still have the chance to get some unique photos tonight."

"Are we crazy for doing this?" Sadie asked. "I mean, do you think this is really going to work?"

Julie cut the shirt into long strips. While she wrapped them around a long oak branch, Caleb offered, "Well, it isn't unprecedented. We have three things going for us." He pointed to a large Apatosaurus that was moving into the falls. It was nibbling on the ferns nesting among the rocks. "First, every major *megafauna* that existed at the same time as people was wiped out by us. Everything from mammoths to saber-toothed tigers. It's only in the last hundred years or so that we've stopped trying to kill large undomesticated beasts. By a pure act of will, elephants and rhinoceroses are still alive."

Sadie and Julie stood on either side of him. They watched the large herbivore slowly make his way through the foliage.

"They are gentle giants, aren't they?" Sadie asked.

"They can all go hug a falling meteor," Julie said hoarsely.

"That's the Playa I know." Caleb laughed. Julie chuckled.

"So what's the second thing?" Sadie asked.

"Predator-prey role reversals. Sometimes in the animal world, prey becomes a predator, and a predator becomes prey. The bison stop and turn and attack the wolf, and they kill the wolf. Some species of larva feed on the frogs that try to eat them. They actually lure the predator to them."

"That sounds familiar," Sadie said.

Caleb continued. "Some herbivores have even from time to time become carnivores, like deer that eat squirrels."

"So you're thinking we can be like the larva that eats the frog or the bison that kills the wolf?" Caleb nodded.

"I like that," Sadie said. "And the third thing?"

Julie laughed grimly, "This T-Rex has never met a Granola. She don't know what's coming!"

11

Lauren was required to make a public apology. This was before people realized that making a bully apologize actually reinforced the behavior.

Before she could make an apology, she first wrote Sadie a letter. This letter was ordered by the courts. In it, Lauren explained that she was wrong and shouldn't have used that word or called her that name. Her lawyer and her parents also had letters explaining how much this crime would affect their loved one's future. "It doesn't make it right," Lauren's mother wrote. "What my daughter said was cruel and horrible and cannot be undone. I didn't raise her that way. But if you press charges, it could ruin her future." The fact that Lauren's mother was the geology teacher, Mrs. Waynewright, only added to the sincerity.

The reality was, Sadie just wanted this to be over. She didn't want to hear again about what Lauren had done or said, and she declined the opportunity to discuss the matter with the high school counselor. She just wanted to move on with her life. So she checked the box saying she wouldn't press charges, despite her parents advising her otherwise.

Principal Matthews wasn't satisfied. This wasn't just an insult to one Senior. He oversaw a multi-racial, international school of over a thousand students. In his opinion, what Lauren said and attempted to do was essentially a hate crime against the entire student body. But this was in the time before the advent of cyberbullying and before the open knowledge that some students were being bullied so horribly that they chose suicide over attending school. His recommendations were not favored by the superintendent. So Principal Matthews mandated to Lauren's parents that Lauren had to make a public apology at the pep rally, or she would be expelled for the rest of the year.

"I'm sorry, everybody," Lauren read from a statement that the family lawyer helped her craft. "What I said, and how I behaved, has embarrassed my school. It was grossly negligent of the school's code of ethics and our creed. It was not Courageous, Intelligent, or Accepting. It was not becoming of a member of the Pride. It was the opposite of that. I especially want to apologize to…Sadine Williams. Nothing can eliminate the stain…" she paused and caught her breath. "The stain on my soul for what I did to you. I'm…I'm sorry." She burst out into tears and rushed off the stage.

Principal Matthews stood up and said, "I speak for Sadine when I say that we want to put this terrible event behind us. Remember, Lions, the immortal words of Mahatma Gandhi: 'Be the change you want to see in the world.' Now let's get on with the pep rally!"

And everybody moved on. Life at West Lake had been irreversibly changed by Homecoming, but it was far from over. The world kept spinning. Years later, what happened would be remembered, then forgotten, then transformed into ephemeral school legend. "That time some students pulled a *Carrie* at Homecoming."

Two weeks after Sadie was nearly bathed in feces, half the student council was busted for smoking pot in the bathroom after school, and suddenly there were bigger problems in the world of West Lake High than Homecoming.

But it wasn't just the small, insular world of West Lake that was changing. In December, an old boogeyman named Saddam Hussein was captured in something called a spider-hole. Later, somebody discovered a website called The Facebook, and that website was kindling to a fire that burned through the student body.

In this way, everybody forgot. Everybody except Lauren, who could never forget, and she decided to wage a one-woman war against Sadie for getting her nearly expelled. She had to change her tactics, but she wouldn't let Sadie forget her place, and she'd make sure everybody remembered.

"Why are you still angry at her?" Kora asked her one day driving home after school. "That's dangerous. You nearly got expelled. If you're just trying to one-up her, you shouldn't worry. A girl like her will never be able to catch up to you."

"She's different, and I don't mean different in a good way like Jake Chun who is a trust fund baby or Eric Younger who is great at football and his parents are on City Council. She's an outsider. She's not from here, and she doesn't know how to wear clothes like a normal person and her skin looks dirty and gross."

"So not like Marcus."

"Marcus Trapp? Ew. He wears hoodies like some gangbanger."

"But he's nice."

"Kora, don't even start thinking like that. Nice? Baby ducks are nice. Writing letters to troops in Afghanistan is nice. But guys like Marcus Trapp and girls like Sadie Fulton are the opposite of nice. They are abominations."

"Can I be honest?"

"You're my best friend. Of course you can."

"That sounds racist. I didn't say anything earlier because it was just against Sadie, but that sounds kind of racist."

"What? I'm not a racist! I'm like the most unracist person ever."

"You used the 'N' word."

Lauren pinched her nose where it met her forehead. "Look, racism is like Jim Crow laws. It's Friends not having a black character except Aisha Tyler. This isn't about her race or Marcus's race or your race or my race. You can be white or black or Asian. I don't care. This is about what is right and wrong, what is decent and indecent. And Sadie Fulton is indecent."

"So she's indecent?"

"Corrupt and indecent. An outsider."

Kora nodded. She could be down with that. Lauren stared crossly out the window of Kora's Mustang.

Lauren stopped leaving bags of dog turds. She had to, so she never left another one. But she made sure the stink lingered on. She enjoyed watching the little Oreo try to find where the smell was coming from, but she'd never find it. Lauren was too sneaky. The smell was much fainter, like somehow just a little pinch of poo was placed in her locker. Or maybe under it? Sadie wouldn't know exactly. She couldn't find the source.

A week later, Lauren walked by her in the hallway. She made sure to address her loudly so that everyone could hear.

"Shit..." she said loudly, then paused with a wicked smile on her face. "...Stain."

She pointed a ringed finger at the Oreo and said, "'Cause you're just a stain on my life," as she laughed loudly. Not as many kids laughed as Lauren wanted, but it got everybody's attention, and after that, she had a new nickname for Sadie, one that she couldn't be expelled for, but everybody knew what she was *really* saying. Sure, that lowlife Caleb and the other Granola Droppings would tell Principal Matthews, and he would admonish her to choose better words, especially after what happened at Homecoming. But he wouldn't expel her. It'd be worth it. Especially because she had much bigger plans for Shit Stain.

12

Sadie hid in the woods at the banks where the Seven Graves River became Dinosaur Falls. If everything went well, she wouldn't need to get wet. She was the backup if anything went wrong between Caleb and Julie. Her primary purpose would be to tap the rocks with her metal hiking pole. The impact was enough to alert Caleb that it was time to spring the trap, assuming he didn't know already. So besides the hiking pole, she carried a pocket knife and bear spray.

Julie volunteered to be the bait, of course. She said it was because she wanted the job where all she had to do was stand. If anything went wrong, the secondary would have to run out into the river, and Julie wasn't running anywhere. But really, it was guilt. If anybody was going to die, she wanted it to be her. She deserved it. This was her plan, her idea. She had procured the information needed to sneak into the park. Ethan may have been the one to convince Caleb and Sadie to do it, but without Julie's resources, this trip would never have happened.

"I'm sorry," Julie said to Caleb once she got to the rock where she was to stand as bait. Caleb had walked her over to the boulders, helping her to keep her balance along the rocks. "This is all my fault."

Before he said anything to lessen her guilt, Julie cut him off. "Don't tell me it's not. I know you want to, but it is my fault."

"*It's an adventure we'll never tell our grandkids about.*"

"Ethan liked saying that any time the trek went south," she said. "But he was also fond of saying, *Anything less than somebody dying is an adventure.* Well, here we are, Caleb. We're just a bunch of high school losers who became a bunch of losers in life. We stupidly tried to reclaim some high school glory by illegally crossing into one of the most dangerous regions on the planet. And now we're paying for it. We're getting exactly what losers deserve."

"We aren't losers."

"*Au contraire*, we were the definition of losers. We skipped school to go hiking and camping. None of us was in the top ten percent of our class. Hell, none of us was in the top twenty five percent. Nobody was Student Body President or even Secretary to the AV Club."

"You weren't in the AV Club."

"Exactly! My parents begged me to join the AV Club or Volleyball or the Spanish Club or anything. I refused every time."

"You refused because it was your parents who were very controlling and unsupportive of the person you wanted to be."

"We. Were. Losers."

"No," Caleb said, hurt in his voice. "We were friends. We had our own club. We were the Granolas. We looked out for each other back then. If anything, what makes us losers is we stopped caring about each other. It took all of us hitting this absolute nadir of life to convince us to come back together. I should have reached out to you much earlier. I should've never lost contact with you in college. I should have hung out with Ethan more."

She sobbed and put her arms around him.

"I was in AV Club, you know."

"I know," she said, as if that wasn't the point at all. It wasn't.

"Do you regret that night in Trinity Alps?"

"No."

Her head was still buried in his shoulder when Caleb said, "You say this all happened because we're losers. I think it's because we're sinners."

Conciliatory, she said, "Everybody owes a life."

"We owe one more."

Julie was always amazed when Caleb's Christian side came out. Most of the time, he was the science-minded man, but every once in a while, she was reminded that he came from a devout religious upbringing. Her parents were also devoted to the Gospels. The difference between her and Caleb was that none of it rubbed off on her. She was okay with the concept of a God as creator, but not okay with the idea that everything was done according to His will, and not hers.

"That was different."

"I'm not so sure. The past can't be undone, but when you do what we did, it stains not just you but your whole life, and there's no coming back from it."

Julie pushed away from Caleb. "Didn't God tell Abraham to kill his son? Weren't there a thousand times in the Bible where God told some tribe to go kill another?"

"God didn't tell us to do that."

"God didn't tell us to come here, either, and look where we are, Caleb. Stop trying to see things that aren't there. We deal with the problem in front of us, and then we deal with the next problem, and then the next if we have to. The minute we try to prescribe meaning to it, we lose our focus. That's how we die."

"You're right, of course."

"Of course I am. But I'm glad it's you guys who are here with me. I'd rather it be you and Bucky than anyone else."

They hugged. In the distance, the T-Rex roared.

"Go. Get into position," she said.

Caleb walked off with the hiking pole. He lay down in a small eddy behind a jagged rock. Completely submerged, he breathed through the hollow hiking pole. The grip at the top had been removed as well as the lower tip, forming a big reed.

Julie situated herself on the collection of boulders at the edge of the falls, ensuring that her footing was true and she wouldn't slip. In her left hand, she carried the torch, burning bright in the night. She hadn't realized how dark it had gotten as the night wore on. Her watch told her it was almost 3am. Nobody was even thinking of being up at this time. Even the night photographers lasted maybe until 11 or midnight. Others would be up early, perhaps at 4:30 or 5. So she didn't expect to be noticed by anyone until almost dawn, with any rescue op happening in those first hours after dawn. By then, all the crepuscular dinosaurs would have come and gone, and she didn't think there'd be anything but their bones to recover.

Up the river, a giant mass moved in the dark.

13

They arrived off a dirt road that the old Camry could barely manage, bumping and scraping along tire ruts that had formed during the previous winter's severe weather. That weather had meant many days skiing and snowshoe hiking in the California mountains, but now spring had arrived, the snow and ice had begun to melt, and it was time to hit the trails again.

Ethan pulled the packs out of the back of Caleb's car. The group had spent the car ride watching YouTube videos and sipping cheap wine that Ethan's older brother bought for them. Each of them a little high off the wine, they grabbed their gear and headed to the Stuart Fork trailhead. They stopped to fill their water bottles and go to the bathroom before starting their trek.

On the first day of their three-day hike, they climbed up into the secluded forest of giant conifers. Despite it being late April, the air under the trees was always chilly, like the area wanted to lie dormant a little longer and keep winter around. Summer would bring heat, and possibly more forest fires like the Sawtooth Fire two years ago. The Sawtooth Fire had devoured six thousand acres before a freak rainstorm put it out. Now the forest smelled vaguely of charcoal, and many of the trees were like grave markers and memorials to where the rest of the forest should be.

"Seniors, man," Ethan said, clapping Caleb on the back. "Class of 2004. I never thought I would've made it this far."

"Go, Lions!" Julie said.

Sadie raised her hands in the air. She was still wearing her West Lake Lions shirt under her backpack.

"I still can't believe you won the game," Julie said.

"I didn't win the game. I don't even play baseball," Sadie replied.

"Wait. So that wasn't you that caught the foul ball so the South Lake bird-head couldn't get an out on Jaden Houser?"

"I caught a foul ball. I'd hardly call that winning the game."

"We were behind, at the bottom of the ninth, and you caught the ball. Otherwise, Jaden Houser is out and West Lake doesn't make the play-offs. On the very next play Jaden hits a double. We win. YOU WON THE GAME!"

"Bucky balls trumps baseballs!" Ethan shouted exuberantly.

She laughed. She also wished she'd met them a year or two ago.

That morning they climbed a thousand feet over five miles. The Stuart Fork raced along their left side. Winter snow overfed the greedy river. At times it positively roared.

The combination of weather and elements had kept the usually busy trails empty. The mountains were theirs to enjoy. Caleb brought a raft and fishing pole for Sapphire Lake. He was hoping to catch a trout to cook on the lake shore. Julie and Sadie were looking to do some heavy communing with nature. Julie had recently taken up yoga after her breakup with Ethan, and naturally Sadie joined her. They planned to practice their sunrise yoga on the peak overlooking the Sapphire and Emerald lakes. Ethan was planning some solo rock climbing along the Sawtooth Ridge. If he had things his way, he'd be climbing next to some of the thin waterfalls that poured off the mountains like avalanches.

First, they had to hike to the lakes. The out-and-backer was a 24-mile trek that took at least one day of hiking to get to the good stuff, which was probably the only thing keeping more hikers off its trails.

In the early evening they arrived at Morris Meadows and made camp. Fifty-foot tall tree trunks, blackened from the forest fires, were incapable of spoiling the Trinity Alps. The mountains rose in granite magnificence all around them. They were in heaven.

As they ate Mountain House spaghetti and chicken dumplings, they watched a second group enter the meadow. At first, they didn't really pay them any attention. They weren't surprised that others would be here, but they were so invested in their own good humor, they didn't think much about the outside world. This was the time in a person's life for celebrating 12 years of education, and becoming an adult. They didn't have the inclination for others.

"Oh my God. Shit Stain, is that you?" Lauren called out. She waved cheerfully from the other side of the meadow, as if she were waving to long lost friends and not a group of people who had written fan fiction plotting the many ways she could die.

"You gotta be kidding me," Julie mumbled. "Of all the trails in all of friggin' California, she has to come to ours?"

Julie stood up and yelled, "You need to leave!"

"What did I do?" Lauren shot back. Her friends appeared at her side, just now coming off the trail. There were seven of them. Besides her besties Kora and Jenna, there was Eric Younger and three of his fellow football players who also doubled on the baseball team. Jaden Houser was one of them.

"We're having a real good time here. Go find another place to camp."

Eric stepped up and said, "Hey, that's not fair. There aren't that many places to camp."

In response, Julie waved her hands all around her.

"Look, you're the ones with all the experience. Why don't you go find a better place? You can probably have a new camp going before we set up."

"That's not the point, and it's not my problem. We planned this months ago." She pointed to their high school packs and the tents carried in their hands. "When did you all decide, this morning?"

Eric marched toward her. Julie was taken aback. She forgot what a big dude he was. There was a reason he made All-Region. Six-foot-two and two-hundred-and-ten pounds of sinewy muscle was a lot to take down, and his arms were as big around as tree trunks, which was saying a lot in northern California.

"Come on," Kora said. "I thought I saw a spot in the woods where we can camp." She tugged on Eric's arm until he followed her.

After Lauren's group walked off, Julie spun around, fuming. "I can't believe them. You know they planned this on purpose."

"Not everything is about us," Caleb said. "I really think they just decided to do some camping in Trinity Alps. Sapphire Lake is real popular. They probably decided at the game to come out here, drink some booze and get laid."

"I don't give a tiny bat's butt crack."

Caleb laughed first. "A tiny what?"

"A tiny bat's butt crack. You've never heard that?"

The tension eased, and they gravitated back into their celebration.

After they finished dinner, Ethan and Julie prepped the bear bag, and Sadie went to the Fork to wash herself off. She hadn't seen any bears, but just the thought that they were out there made her nervous. She wanted to make sure there wasn't any chicken dumpling scent on her that would make a bear want to break into her tent just to get a taste.

She brought the camp soap with her and made sure to soak her arms up to the elbows. She scrubbed hard.

"You know, you can't wash that out, Bucky," Eric said as he came up beside her. He had a tin cup and cooking pan in his hands as well as a wash rag and a bottle of soap.

Sadie's eyes knitted together angrily. Her entire body tensed up. She set her jaw.

"Naw, it ain't like that, girl. I mean the scent of your food. That's what you're trying to get off, right? I can see you're trying to wash it off so hard you almost washed yourself red. But if you haven't got it yet, nothing will."

"I don't like you." Those four words weren't the worst insult the world ever came up with, but they were the most direct, and that was enough for her. She was almost shocked to hear the words coming out of her mouth. Sadie had to suppress the urge to cover her mouth with her hands. Instead, she capped off the camp soap and walked away.

"Why you gotta be like that?"

"Be like what?" Inside, a portion of her was yelling to shut up and keep walking. *You don't act like this!* the voice yelled. The people who spoke out got in trouble. Or worse, they got bullied. If she'd just stop talking, he'd go away.

He sighed. "Look, I know this doesn't seem fair."

"Fair? How could you be seen with that bigot?"

He looked down on her like she was a child being explained the rules of the game. "Life isn't easy, buttercup. It never is. And while Lauren does have a wild side, and she doesn't always think things through before the words come out of her mouth, she isn't wrong, either."

Sadie stood in shock. Words failed her.

Eric laughed jovially. Sadie wondered what great joke he was about to share.

"She doesn't like you because of what you represent, not because of who you are."

"Enlighten me."

"You're like those poseur white kids who want to act black. They talk like us and dress like us, but they aren't black."

"Eric, I'm black. Nobody in my family came across on the Mayflower. My line crossed from Africa on slave ships just like you."

"No, you don't get it. That's not what I'm trying to say. Your father, he's black. And your mama, too. But you? Girl, you're white. It's like that Eddie Murphy skit. You know the one? He's a black man, and one day he goes undercover as a white dude. He can buy whatever he wants, get loans for free, and everywhere is a cocktail party with pretty women. Now, I know what you're going to say. But the reality is that your skin is too light. And look at how you dress. You dress white. So maybe you aren't white, but you're sure as hell not black, and you sure as hell don't have my problems or the problems of anyone else. Look at me. I'm in AP classes, yet when I walk into a white store, people wonder if I'm going to rob the place. People don't look at you the same way. That sounds awful, and I'm sorry I have to be the one to tell you this, but it's the reality. You don't have a black person's problems or their culture."

Sadie had curled her fists into balls. She didn't know if she wanted to cry or get angry. She wanted to do both, actually. But she was like an engine that couldn't decide between reverse and first gear. She was stuck in her clutch.

"So, yeah, what Lauren did was over the top. No white person should be calling a black person nigger. But she was reminding you of where you come from. Maybe if you hadn't forgotten your roots, you wouldn't have this problem."

"Fine!" she shouted. "Either I'm too white or I'm too black. Which one is it, 'cause it can't be both."

He held his hands up like he was dealing with a lost cause. "You want to blame me. I had nothing to do with it."

"You accepted it. When you had the chance, you were on her side."

"All sides are wrong in this case."

"No, that isn't true."

He shrugged as if to say, you can't talk to some people. "I'm not part of this. I just wanted to tell you what truth looks like. Keep it real for you. And it's not Lauren you should be worried about. At least Lauren was upfront with you. Caleb, though. That Benedict Arnold's been stabbing you in the back since you got here."

"What?"

He chortled. "That's right. You don't know. Look, I'm out. I'm sorry for you, really I am. Have a nice weekend."

He walked away toward his camp and left Sadie fuming, tears streaming down her face. But now she wasn't just angry. She was hurt.

Ethan saw Sadie first. She shook as she walked back to camp.

"Bucky? What's wrong?" Immediately, his head swiveled around, checking out the other camp. "Did Lauren do something?"

Sadie stayed resolute. She walked into camp. Everybody had jumped up and circled around her, asking her what was going on. Clearly, something had happened, and they were ready to go to war. Sadie glowered at Caleb, burning a hole into his face.

"What?" he asked. Then realization surfaced on his face. His body crumpled.

Sadie slapped him hard across the face. Caleb's glasses flew off.

"How could you?" She punched him in the stomach. He didn't defend himself. He went down hard. She tried to kick him, but Ethan pulled her away.

"Stop it, Sadie. What's going on?"

"It was him! He's the one who put those bags in my locker!"

"Caleb? No way. Caleb likes you more than any of us." Ethan said. Julie just stared back in dismay.

"I bet you were in on the whole thing," Sadie said. Her voice was so low, she was practically growling at Caleb. "That's why you agreed to go to Homecoming with me. You were in on it with Lauren. You helped her do that to me!"

"No! I didn't know she was planning anything. I only went because you asked me."

"And afterward? When the smell lingered in my locker? That was you, too, wasn't it?"

"I didn't put it in there, I swear."

"Liar!" She tried to kick him again. He rolled away.

Ethan picked Sadie up off the ground and pulled her away. None of this made sense to him or Julie. Ethan needed to pull his friends apart so that they could understand what was happening.

In a very even voice, Julie said, "Tell us what's going on, Caleb."

Caleb collected his glasses and his body off the meadow floor. His clothes were covered in grass seeds and pine cones.

"I hacked into the computer system. I gave Lauren the locker combinations."

"What? You? Aw, man…" Ethan cringed. "How could you?"

"You're a monster!" Sadie yelled.

Julie watched in horror. "You're supposed to be the good kid."

"After all those times that we sat around trying to come up with who it was, it was you?" Ethan said. "How could you do that?"

"Yes," Sadie said, her voice as cold as ice. "Tell us why you helped somebody you profess to hate."

Julie interjected. "No. That's alright. We don't need to know. You should leave, Caleb. Go away."

Caleb looked at the angry faces of his best friends, the people he'd betrayed. He took his pack and hefted it on his shoulders.

"I'm sorry," he offered.

"Go!" Sadie shot back.

Caleb walked out of camp. It was night.

14

Julie and Ethan carried on about Caleb until after nightfall. They were all in shock that their friend could betray them. At one point, Julie cried out, "I hope you fall off a mountain, Caleb!"

Sadie left the camp.

"Where are you going?" Julie asked.

"I just need some time alone," Sadie said. "I'll be back in a minute."

Sadie walked into the trees. With the full moon, she didn't need a flashlight to see around. Caleb's tracks were obvious. They had a distinct star shape in the center of the heel that made him easy to track. He was obviously taking the trail back to his car. She wondered briefly about getting a ride home. Maybe Ethan's older brother could come pick them up if he wasn't working.

She heard a grunt and the sound of something falling in the bushes. Caleb's tracks led in that direction, so she pushed the bushes aside. Flashlights crisscrossed in front of her, spotlighting Caleb. He was without his pack, and he was hunched over on his knees. Jaden and Trent stood over him, chuckling.

"What are you doing?" Sadie asked.

"Bucky, walk away," Caleb said.

Sadie paused. She always walked away. That was how she avoided trouble. Hadn't her parents told her to walk away from fights when she could? And neither Trent nor Jaden had any beef with her.

"Just walk away," Caleb insisted, but it was too late.

"Well, well," Lauren said. "We're going to have some fun now."

Sadie turned to run, but Eric and Kora grabbed her. They forced her to Lauren. Lauren's smile was full of devilish intentions.

15

The T-Rex smiled at Julie fiendishly. A long scar ran down the side of her nose, a reminder of some long-since defeated foe. Where the scar met that sick smile, the teeth were missing. Whatever fought the T-Rex, if it died fighting the T-rex, it hadn't gone down without a fight and leaving some worthwhile damage.

Julie hadn't really looked at the T-Rex since the dinosaur began chasing them on the other side of the sunset. Now that Julie had the opportunity, she wished she hadn't. The T-Rex's face was utterly gruesome. One eye drooped lower than the other like it was melted. Another set of scars told Julie that this dinosaur had fought many battles. She was missing one of the fingers in her forelimbs, on the left hand. Parasitic worms wiggled from the top of her head where the Tyrannosaur could not reach them. Julie wanted to throw up.

The battle-scarred dinosaur ambled slowly up the river, her head nosing left and right.

Julie concentrated hard on not pissing her pants. There was nothing between her and this monster, and she was holding a torch to get her attention.

"H-h-h-ey!" Julie stammered. She steeled herself and shouted, "Over here, ugly!" She waved her torch at the dinosaur. The T-Rex stopped and watched her for a moment.

"Come on!"

The T-Rex sniffed the river below.

"No, no sniffing. Come to me! Delicious Julie! I'm ready to be eaten!"

The dinosaur's tail weaved back and forth. The T-Rex lowered her head and released a giant roar that nearly knocked Julie off the rocks. Then the T-Rex stalked the river banks.

"No. Over here!"

But the Tyrannosaur completely ignored Julie. The T-Rex worked the far side of the river, turning over rocks that were way too heavy for any human to lift, but the giant made short work of it with her fierce claws. She flipped the rocks, then sniffed the scent pulled up from underneath the rock. Once she was satisfied with the odor she'd found, the T-Rex ravaged the next large rock.

"She's trailing Bucky," Julie realized. She didn't notice she was talking out loud.

"She's trailing Bucky!" Julie yelled. She waved her torch over the water, trying to get Caleb's attention, but he was behind a rock and couldn't see the glow of the fire. She kicked the rocks and the water. Pain crisscrossed along her chest. She finally jumped in the water. The pain was enough to knock her over. She inhaled the pain and curled her arms toward her body. Grunting, she forced her way to Caleb. As she rounded the rock he was behind, he jumped up out of the cold water.

"Bucky, run!" Julie shouted.

16

The two athletes dragged Sadie and Caleb deep into the woods. Rain pelted the tree branches overhead. Sadie could smell the fresh pine all around her, but there was something else in the air. The intent. This had been a trap disguised as a coincidence. She could smell their anger and hatred like it was something that aerated out of the pores in their skin.

Down in a copse of dead trees, they lashed Sadie and Caleb down. Caleb writhed as they worked his hands and feet into the loops. It took Jaden, Trent, Eric, and Kora to keep him down. Jenna and the last ball player, David, held on to Sadie so she couldn't run. After Caleb was tied to the stakes buried in the ground, they secured Sadie, too.

Lauren kneeled next to Sadie. "You have been a pain in my ass since the day you arrived, Shit Nigger. Can I say that? Are you okay with that?"

"Hey," Eric said. He was standing akimbo next to some small barrels.

"PC police," Lauren said, rolling her eyes. "That's the problem with the world today. We get bothered by words. And words are just words. They can't do any real harm. But I'm going to correct that tonight, Shit Stain."

She still said it with that deliberate pause.

"Let us go," Caleb said. His wet hair and clothes were plastered to his skin.

"Oh, why would I do that to two worthless turds such as yourselves? The world is better off without you."

To Sadie, Lauren asked, "Now that the cat's out of the bag, did Caleb tell you how I blackmailed him?"

Sadie refused to respond.

"I caught him screwing my mom. That's why he got me those combinations, and that's why he told me you all would be here tonight."

"It wasn't like that," Caleb said.

"Yes it was, you son of a bitch. You deserve everything that's coming to you and then some. That's what real justice looks like. When people are held responsible for their actions."

"What about you?" Caleb said. "Who's holding you accountable?"

"When you've been wronged as deeply as I have, you gain this ability. It's kind of like a blind kid who hears real well or an autistic savant. Any sense of remorse was pulled out of my soul when I caught you and Mom after school."

"She made me do that. I didn't have a choice."

"You always have a choice."

"She was abusing me, Lauren. It was wrong."

"Wrong is carving up my home life and gifting me nightmares of my parents breaking up and my Mom losing her job. Wrong is a sanctimonious Oreo who thinks she can have whatever she wants. Who thinks her shit don't stink. Well, does it now, Shit Stain?"

Still, Sadie refused to say anything.

"So, we are going to have us a little party tonight. I am going to erase the two biggest stains in my life. I am going to wash you two out, and when I do, I will finally be clean again. Now, you may be asking your demented little selves how I am going to wash your stains away. Well, it takes a really hard cleanser to do that. Fortunately, I was able to nab some from the chemistry lab. Trent and David made sure to get it up here for me. Thank you, boys."

They nodded grimly. They were ready to see some action. They wanted to see meat squirm.

"Safety first," Lauren said. She put on safety glasses and vinyl gloves. Then she opened one of the barrels and scooped a white powder into a large pill box so that it was sheltered from the rain.

She walked over to Sadie first. She pulled Sadie's shirt up, exposing her to the rain. "Normally, I need water for this, but with this downpour, Mother Nature's working with me."

She traced her finger along Sadie's belly. "Do you know what lye is? It's a chemical used in making soap, but my dad also uses it when Animal Control needs to dispose of roadkill. They douse the armadillo or dog or whatever it is with lye, soak it in water for a couple of hours, and all that comes out is brown goop."

"Stop what you're doing," Caleb said. "Right now, all you've done is threaten us, but if you do this, there's no going back."

"Oh, Caleb, this has been set in stone for a long time. It's like it was destined in the stars."

"Let Sadie go!"

"Hush. I'll be over there soon, and we'll take care of your pecker. I wonder how it shrivels up in lye."

Caleb thrashed about. Jaden punched him across the side of the mouth.

Gently, Lauren tapped the pill box over Sadie's belly. Flakes of lye fell out. It felt like baby powder. But then it began to burn on her wet belly, small at first, like a mosquito bite, but then it grew. Red splotches formed on her skin. Sadie gritted her teeth.

"Come on, Shit Stain. Don't fail me now. Squirm, girl," Lauren said. She kept running the lye in loops around her belly and then over Sadie's breasts. "We're going to clean you up real good, Shit Stain. You won't be able to bother anyone after this."

Sadie grimaced. Tears streamed out of her eyes. She fought back the urge to scream. She wouldn't give them that satisfaction.

Lauren watched her fight against the burn, then she turned to Caleb and pulled down his pants and underwear. Jenna and Kora giggled. The guys grumbled. They couldn't watch.

"That limp thing is not going to do," Lauren said. "I've got an idea. Since you liked it so much when my mom jerked you off..." she dusted the palms of her gloves in lye.

17

Sadie stood frozen to her spot at the edge of the falls. Upstream, the terrible dinosaur had stopped approaching Julie and began overturning rocks. Sadie wondered, if she moved, would the T-Rex see her? Was the dinosaur really smelling Sadie, or was she sniffing other creatures, maybe fish or crustaceans? A part of her wanted to believe the dinosaur wasn't after her. There was too much risk in giving herself away. But this ugly mother dino had tracked them for miles across a national park and down a river. There was no way she wasn't hunting them.

The admission that they were being hunted burned inside Sadie. She wasn't being chased. This wasn't hide and seek as a kid. The end of this road, however much longer this road extended, ended with either Sadie escaping or the T-Rex eating her. *How had she let this happen?* Sadie wondered. The thought was purely instinctual. She knew how this had happened. In some ways, it was a path that she had been locked into when she went to Homecoming or Trinity Alps.

Julie began yelling and waving at the T-Rex. The T-Rex glanced at her, then returned her attention back to the rocks. Her tail waved behind her eagerly.

As strange as it was to be tracked by certain death, something even more implausible happened. She heard Ethan's voice. She knew it must be in her head because Ethan was dead, and there was no coming back from death. That was one of the truisms that she'd learned the hard way. There was no coming back. So the voice in her head couldn't be Ethan's. And yet, there it was, yelling at her. "Run! Run!"

Sadie grabbed the hiking pole and ran back into the trees. Behind her, the sound of Tyrannosaurus steps thundered along the riverbed. With each pulverizing thud, Sadie stifled a scream.

Whum!

Whum!

Whum!

Sadie leaped over a large tree root in her path and ducked under a tree limb. She zig-zagged between several black pines before putting her hand on a large black spear-tip of a tree and hiding behind it. She turned to see what happened to the T-Rex. The forest had gone silent.

The Rex was standing still. She'd lumbered into the forest of dead trees, and now she was scanning side to side with her colossal head. Branches snapped in the wake of the T-rex's movement. The worms on her head undulated slowly in the wind as if caught in a trance. The T-Rex sniffed a tree, then used her massive feet to push it over. The giant tree cracked and splintered under her weight. She sniffed around the tree, then faced Sadie.

Sadie held her breath. She couldn't stop her body from shuddering, though. It started in her neck and splayed out along her arms and legs.

The Tyrannosaurus Rex cocked her head to one side. Slowly, she took another step forward and stopped. Her tail, normally weaving back and forth, lifted and stayed as still and straight as an arrow. The tip of the arrow, the dinosaur's head, pointed directly at the tree Sadie was hiding behind.

Sadie wished her heart would stop banging like a machine gun in her chest. In a moment that lasted forever, the T-Rex contemplated the next move.

Sadie focused on her quaking fear. Her shivering was getting worse. Her arms and legs vibrated in grotesque spasms.

Stop it! Sadie commanded, but her extremities continued to convulse uncontrollably.

Suddenly, something large crashed in the woods. The T-Rex didn't move. She snorted and waited.

Sadie knew she was in a stalemate with an apex predator, and that the Rex was waiting for her to move first. That's all it would take. She'd watched enough nature shows to know that if she moved, she was done. And yet, her arms began shaking with fear. She wanted to bolt and find another hiding place.

That large nose dipped closer to Sadie. Gently, the dinosaur prodded the ground in front of the tree. She sniffed the base of the burnt tree. She opened her foul mouth and licked Sadie's tracks. Her teeth were eight-inch long sickles, yellowed and blood-stained. Three were missing. One was growing back. Her breath smelled like the insides of a thousand dead animals.

A hiking boot rolled out of her mouth. Sadie clapped her hands over her mouth and rolled onto her butt. She recognized Ethan's boots from the last three days of backpacking. Every night Ethan left his old, worn out boots outside his tent, and every morning, Sadie unzipped her tent screen and was greeted by the sight of his boots across the campsite. Unlike hers, Ethan's boots were crumpled and well-used. The top of his boots leaned to one side, the stiffness worn out of them.

It made sense that the T-Rex would find Ethan's corpse if it was tracking them, and as an opportunity predator, it made sense that the T-Rex would consume whatever remained of Ethan. Logically, this all made sense. But emotionally, nothing was right. Ethan shouldn't be dead, and they shouldn't be on the falls.

The T-Rex cocked her head to one side. Didn't move.

Sadie reached to her side, her fingers trembling. She tried to make as little noise as possible as she pulled the bear spray from her belt strap. She had no idea whether the spray worked on dinosaurs, but it was her only remaining option. The spray can tugged at her belt but didn't release. She glanced between the Rex and the bottle. The T-Rex sniffed the exact spot where she had touched the tree.

She reminded herself not to overreact. Things happen. If you overreact, you just get the bully's attention, whether it is in high school, college, at work, or being chased by a dinosaur. She relaxed her grip, then tried a different direction for moving the spray can out of its holster. It still wasn't coming out.

The giant mouth full of death slowly moved around the tree.

Sadie jerked the bottle hard. It finally released. She remembered reading the directions for using the bear spray. There was a safety and a trigger, and the bear needed to be at least a few feet away. She would have to make due.

The T-Rex struck. Sadie screamed as she unleashed a torrent of bear spray on the T-Rex.

18

Caleb helped Julie steady herself in the water. She handed him the torch. "I'll be fine. Go help Bucky!"

Torch in one hand, axe in the other, Caleb pushed through the surging water and up onto a small beach. On the beach, he plunged into the night, searching for the Tyrannosaurus Rex. He was surprised at how easily the dinosaur moved through the conifer forest. Like a giant Siberian Tiger stalking its prey in the underbrush, the T-Rex left relatively few signs. For something so big, he would have expected more damage.

He held his torch out, but only black lines in a shadowy, scary world appeared in his torchlight. He stopped moving and tried to listen as intently as possible, closing his eyes and concentrating on the sounds of the forest. If Sadie was hiding, he wouldn't be able to hear her. But he should be able to hear the Rex. Right?

Something moved in the distance to his left. Slowly, he walked under a canopy of dead trees looking for the T-Rex. He wondered what he would do when he found the monster. He needed a strategy of some sort. He decided that animals feared fire, so he would push the flames and hope that did enough. If it didn't, he'd strike her with the axe. He'd only have one shot, so he'd have to make it count. Maybe go for the eyes? That wouldn't work. The eyes were too far away. He needed an easy target.

The belly? That could work.

The dinosaur made a heavy sound as it moved. Caleb distinctly made out the shift from one foot to the other, and for the first time it dawned on him that the T-Rex may not be after Sadie anymore and may actually be hunting him. This thought made the hairs on the back of his neck stand up.

He'd need to more careful. Should he douse the fire?

No, if (*when*) the dinosaur attacked, that'd be his best defense.

He stepped lightly through the forest, hoping the dinosaur wouldn't hear him moving. His eyes blazed wide open, trying to capture any shape or movement, anything to key him off that the T-Rex was near.

Suddenly, a large creature longer than a crocodile with a tall sail on its back chomped at Caleb. Caleb shrieked. Thwack! He hit the Dimetrodon with as much power as he could muster. The camp axe connected with the dinosaur's back. The Dimetrodon thrashed back and forth, knocking over several ashen logs as it tried to escape Caleb. Caleb was now more afraid that he would lose his axe, so he put his boot onto the dinosaur's shoulder and heaved back. The axe came loose, and he fell on his back, hitting his head hard enough to make him dizzy.

The Dimetrodon stopped spinning. Its face was now almost on top of Caleb. He dared not move. The creature hissed angrily, then ran off into the underbrush.

From deeper in the forest, he heard a scream.

Caleb struggled to get to his feet. He'd nearly been killed by the small predator. Now it was time to find the big one.

19

Ethan punched Jaden hard across the side of the head. He'd come running silently out of the trees. Ethan knew the best place to hit somebody was in the temple. Jaden fell down unconscious.

The other players jumped him. Ethan got a few hits in, but they beat him silly until he was a bloody mess in the ground. In the scrum, his bag of M&Ms fell apart and spilled onto the forest floor.

Lauren's attention had shifted to the fight. Once it was over, she went back to Caleb and his uncoiled manhood.

"Go away!" Ethan yelled through his bloody mouth. "Leave us alone."

Their fear was palpable in the late night air.

Kora and Jenna giggled. One of them said, "Shut up, faggot."

Lauren said, "That's right. So we have the losers here but one. The faggot, the teacher fiddler, and the Oreo. Where's the Banana?"

A metal tip sliced through the beams of moonlight. It swiped across Eric's face, cutting his cheek open. He screamed as he fell to his knees.

"Right here, and I'm full of potassium!" Julie yelled. She carried one of Ethan's metal climbing picks in each hand.

As Trent and Jaden reached for her, Ethan tripped them up. He punched Jaden with his whole body, then collapsed in exhaustion. It was all the time Julie needed. She sliced through the ropes, releasing Caleb and Sadie. Caleb grabbed a water bottle from out of a nearby pack and squirted the water on Sadie, flushing the lye off her skin. Ravaged, blistered skin remained in its wake.

The four friends backed up near a pine with a base as thick around as a dining table. Julie stood in the front, her green-dyed hair burning bright in the darkness. She held the climbing picks like sickles. Caleb and Ethan stood behind her, and Sadie remained in the back where she couldn't be hurt.

20

Sadie kept pumping her legs. Every time she hid behind a tree, the T-Rex thoughtfully followed her to that tree and found her. The giant predator would then either use her expansive claws to push over the dead tree or, if the tree was too thick or still alive, she would poke her head covered in wiggling worms around the trunk and snap at Sadie, who would then plug the T-rex's face full of bear spray and run. The T-rex would shake the spray off and continue her pursuit.

It was a game of hide and seek with deadly consequences to the loser.

The last time, the spray ran out halfway through its burst.

Sadie screamed.

As the T-Rex's head pulled away, Sadie ran around the tree and circled back. She bolted for the river. Her head was coming back to her. If she could make it to the river, her friends could help her. Caleb had the axe. The plan could still work. The only thing that changed was that she was the bait now, not Julie.

She knew the river's location by the sound of the falls rushing over its ledge of granite and limestone.

Sadie hurtled through an obstacle course of fallen trees and sunken stones to the river. Halfway between the falls and the riverbank stood Julie. With her ribs fractured, Julie was struggling to push through the headwaters.

"She's right behind me!" Sadie yelled. She waved her hands at her sides. "Get away!"

Julie yelled something to her, but Sadie was so focused on the plan, she didn't hear Julie at all. Sadie burst through the trees and out into the Seven Graves. Legs churning, she surged through the riverbed. Her heart was pounding so loud in her chest, she couldn't separate it from the sound of the Tyrannosaurus Rex stomping after her. The Rex had legs like a locomotive that seethed with absolute power.

Sadie jumped on top of Julie's rock while pivoting to face the terror behind her. As she twisted, she lost her footing on the algae. She slid off the rock and tumbled over the falls.

21

Caleb rushed through a copse of trees. The long night had taken its toll on his body, but he didn't have the time to pay it any attention. His friends were in trouble, and he owed them this at least. Didn't his life depend on them? Hadn't they saved him enough times over the years? And even if that wasn't true, there was this simple truth: he had betrayed them. He was their Judas. Everything that happened to them was all his fault. That's where Julie was wrong. It couldn't be her fault. She planned the trip to rekindle something in their lives, that former glory. But if he hadn't helped Lauren, they would all be better people.

It was obvious to him that all their shortcomings began that night in the forest. Julie struggled with finishing anything after that. She'd attended half a dozen colleges before finally graduating. Every year like clockwork he would be invited to like a company on Facebook or LinkedIn or Instagram or wherever. And every time, without fail, the business went under. There was always an excuse, but Caleb knew why she had a hard time finishing things.

Ethan accomplished even less. For all his escapades and his confidence, he spent his nights alone. Something was preventing him from really connecting with people. And all that travel? He never left a hundred mile radius, and he NEVER returned to the Trinity Alps wilderness.

And poor Sadie, she was covered in the physical scars of her trauma. Those tattoos were signs of deeper battles going on inside her head, battles that would eventually tear her apart if she didn't get professional help.

All this because one coward betrayed his friends. He didn't do it for 30 pieces of silver. No, he did it for freedom from guilt. Murder was not the sin he was repaying. It was betrayal of friendship.

That night wouldn't have happened if he hadn't given Lauren the updated locker combinations. But it was worse than that. There was another secret he'd never told them. Lauren knew they'd be there that weekend because he'd told her. Him.

Only the lowest level of hell was reserved for betrayers. He'd been living in it for over a decade. He'd tried to make life work, somehow force the round peg through the square hole of his betrayal, but once a cheater, always a cheater. He was stuck in this cycle. His chance to escape it was Dinosaur Falls.

So he ran at the T-Rex, axe raised high, screaming.

22

Julie watched her friend go over the edge of the falls. She screamed for her.

She'd already lost so much. She refused to lose anyone else. So Bucky didn't know it, but she didn't have a choice in the matter. She would have to be alive. Julie *willed* it so. Either Bucky went over the falls and survived to Banion's Mistake, or she was still hanging from a rock. Those were literally the only two options Bucky was allowed.

If anyone was surviving this, it was Bucky. Not because of what she'd endured through her life, but because of all of them who'd been spit through that sausage grinder of a night, Bucky was the one who handled it the best. She went to one college, a full blown university, and she graduated! She got a job, and she moved through the ranks like anyone else. She had a steady paycheck. She'd never been fired. She'd won awards. She was a good employee. She was everything Julie wished she could be.

If Bucky didn't deserve to live, nobody did.

She slipped on one of the rocks and fell to her hands and knees. She was in too much pain to stand up, so she fought the current from her hands and knees, crawling over the rocks.

A large shadow crossed the moonlight behind her.

She turned her head.

The T-Rex stood over her, tail waving behind her like a flag on an easy-breezy day, the kind of day when the flag really unfurls and makes a popping sound as it tightens against the wind.

The T-Rex reached out to grab her prey.

From the corner of the river, Caleb charged the T-Rex. He hefted the little axe high over his head and chopped the ankles of the Tyrannosaur, burying the blade deep.

Blood spurted from the wound.

The Rex roared something unholy and metallic, but she did not drop to her side like they'd hoped.

The T-Rex swiveled about. As she spun, her leg struck Caleb. He flew twenty feet to the falls and slammed hard into the large, flat rock in the center of the falls, the same one Bucky had gone over. As he struck the rocks, his head snapped back hard. The camping axe slipped out of his hand and skipped off the rock and over the falls.

Julie hadn't stopped crawling to the flat rock. She got there and checked on Caleb. Heavy-lidded eyes tracked her movements as his head rolled toward her. His jaw hung limply from his mouth. There was lots of blood on the rock.

She patted him and crawled to the edge of Dinosaur Falls and looked over the drop fifty feet below to the rocky bottom and gasped. No way anyone could survive that, but that left one option. Julie scanned right, then left. Bucky was clinging to a rock by one hand not three feet over the ledge. In the other hand, she held the axe.

"Bucky!" Julie shouted. Bucky didn't respond. She needed all her strength to keep the rushing waters from hurling her to her death. Julie reached over and grabbed her by the wrist. With everything she had left, she heaved. She literally felt a rib splitting and running up the side of her skin. Now it was a complete break.

Julie and Bucky fell back on the rock. Julie coiled in pain, but Bucky was beside her, no longer in danger of falling, and that's all that really mattered.

"Run," Julie moaned. It was all she had left, and this was the end. She was going to fulfill her promise to be the bait.

23

"Give her up, and we'll let you go," Lauren growled. She stood with the jocks and the mean girls. "You're outnumbered, and you're cornered. All I really want is Stain," she said, pointing at Sadie.

"Come on," Eric said. "Just walk away. Do the smart thing for once."

Ethan glanced back at his friends. They nodded. Ethan purred, "Why start doing the smart thing now?" Then he kicked Eric in the balls so hard that the all-region quarterback dropped like a rock in still waters.

The shadow moved over Bucky. An angry god roared its heavy metal hatred.

Sadie stood resolute on the rock, the axe in her hand. "Why start doing the smart thing now?"

The giant mouth came down on her as she rushed into its cavern of teeth.

The tongue shot forward. Little wormy parasites had attached to the tongue as well. Teeth came down around her. Moonbeams disappeared.

But all Bucky saw was that ugly damn tongue. All those little parasites reaching for her. She brought the axe down on the tongue at the base just as the teeth were starting to press against her skin.

The T-Rex shot back up. Blood rained down on Bucky. For a brief moment, time stopped. Moonbeams broke around the silhouette of the Tyrannosaurus Rex as she arched her back and howled in pain. The tongue hung in the air, almost as if some higher power was levitating it. Black ink spots sprawled over her head like gore shot from a trumpet.

She was mighty.

And then, the moment was over. Shots echoed against the waterfall. Helicopters buzzed overhead. A rescue line lowered to Bucky.

24

Jaden pulled a switchblade from his back pocket. It was an old butterfly, which he flashed in the moonlight and the rain. He swiped across Caleb's stomach, leaving a thin red line in his stomach.

Julie stabbed Jaden with the ice pick. When she pulled it out, blood seeped from Jaden's side, and he fell over.

Kora and Jenna screamed and fled. Lauren reached for the blade. Julie stabbed her in the neck.

Lauren tried to say something, but instead of words, blood gurgled from her mouth. She died somewhere between her knees buckling and her head hitting the piney earth.

Eric and Trent retreated into the forest.

"What do we do now?" Sadie asked.

"We go hunting," Ethan said as Julie tossed him an ice pick.

Caleb picked up the switchblade. "There can't be any survivors, or we all go to jail."

No further discussion was needed among them. They moved like a pack through the forest, chasing down the survivors one by one. Kora was the easiest to catch. She had fallen down into a ball of sorrow and fear. They stabbed her eight times with their makeshift weapons.

Jenna hid from them in the bushes, but she had a distinct heart shape on her footprint. Ethan went around and ahead of Jenna. Caleb and Julie took the sides. Then Sadie ran at the bush, yelling. She flushed her out. Jenna went left, saw Julie, ran right, discovered Caleb, and fled straight into Ethan's climbing pick.

Trent and Eric they found down in a creek by the river. They were harder to take down. They were screaming for help, and they stood back to back. The hunters took turns jumping at them and wearing them down. Finally, Trent stumbled on a rock. Julie and Ethan pounced, sickles drawn. One sickle caught Trent in the side, the other in his face.

"Oh, Gawd, no!" Eric shouted as he backpedaled into Julie, who kicked him in the side hard enough to knock him down. He kept crawling.

"Please, I'm begging you. I didn't mean anything. I didn't know that they were going to come after you. Please, please. I just want to see my mom and dad again. Please," he whimpered.

The hunters jumped on him, claws first.

They dragged the corpses back to the site. Eric was stumbling away, his body still tucked under itself. Ethan had really kicked him hard in the balls.

Sadie tapped Ethan on the shoulder. He handed her the pick. She jogged up beside Eric. The quarterback saw her coming and started to run, but his groin didn't want to cooperate. She easily caught up to him. She stabbed him first in the arm, and then in the hip. She felt the blade of the pick glance off his hipbone. Eric collapsed.

"No, S...S...S..."he tried to say, but there was too much pain for his words. She cut him across the abdomen. His guts rippled out of his skin. Finally, Eric screamed. He got up to a crawling position, but his intestines fell out. He kept pushing forward. She stepped on his guts. It felt rubbery. Eric dragged himself another five feet before he died. Later, Caleb came and retrieved Eric's body.

They piled the bodies on a blue camping tarp and dumped the lye out over them. They let the rain do its work. They built five campfires around the bodies to increase the performance of the lye. It took all night, but by morning they were nothing but pulpy flesh and brittle bones.

Caleb pumped his raft full of air while Ethan scooped the remains into the bucket. Caleb paddled out into the middle of Sapphire Lake and emptied the bucket. It took ten trips to complete the job. On the eleventh trip, he began dropping gear, including their own.

They walked out of the wilderness in fresh clothes, flip flops, and IDs. They never spoke about it again until Ethan reached out years later, asking if they'd go with him and Julie into a savage park full of the most terrible creatures on the planet.

But they all knew the truth. Dinosaurs may have returned to this planet, but there had always been more terrible creatures walking the earth.

The End

Photo by Sam Shepherd

Thanks for Reading
If you enjoyed Backpacking with Dinosaurs, I hope you leave a review on Amazon. Like many authors, I depend on reviews and the referrals of readers. Your support is greatly appreciated.

I am also the author of these fine books:

Severed Press Books by Doug Goodman
Wendigo Road
Dominion
Kaiju Fall
Kaijunaut
Shark Toothed Grin

Zombie Dog Series
Cadaver Dog (Book 1)
Dead Dog (Book 2)
Zombie Dog (Book 3)
Ghost Dog (Book 4, available Spring 2019)

My website is dgoodman1.wordpress.com. Feel free to e-mail me at douggoodmannet@gmail.com. To sign up to be notified of new releases, giveaways, and other book news, check out my website or click here to sign up for the mailing list.

In case you are looking for a few other ways to reach me, here are my social media contacts. I'd love to hear from you.

Facebook: Doug Goodman
Twitter: @DougGoodman1
Instagram: 42Trails or TexasGeekDad
Pinterest: douggoodman

CHECK OUT OTHER GREAT DINOSAUR BOOKS

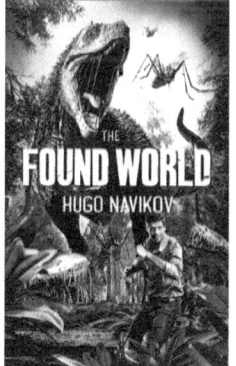

THE FOUND WORLD
by **Hugo Navikov**

A powerful global cabal wants adventurer Brett Russell to retrieve a superweapon stolen by the scientist who built it. To entice him to travel underneath one of the most dangerous volcanoes on Earth to find the scientist, this shadowy organization will pay him the only thing he cares about: information that will allow him to avenge his family's murder.

But before he can get paid, he and his team must enter an underground hellscape of killer plants, giant insects, terrifying dinosaurs, and an army of other predators never previously seen by man.

At the end of this journey awaits a revelation that could alter the fate of mankind ... if they can make it back from this horrifying found world.

HOUSE OF THE GODS
by **Davide Mana**

High above the steamy jungle of the Amazon basin, rise the flat plateaus known as the Tepui, the House of the Gods. Lost worlds of unknown beauty, a naturalistic wonder, each an ecology onto Itself, shunned by the local tribes for centuries. The House of the Gods was not made for men.

But now, the crew and passengers of a small charter plane are about to find what was hidden for sixty million years.

Lost on an island in the clouds 10.000 feet above the jungle, surrounded by dinosaurs, hunted by mysterious mercenaries, the survivors of Sligo Air flight 001 will quickly learn the only rule of life on Earth: Extinction.

CHECK OUT OTHER GREAT DINOSAUR BOOKS

FLIPSIDE
by JAKE BIBLE

The year is 2046 and dinosaurs are real.

Time bubbles across the world, many as large as one hundred square miles, turn like clockwork, revealing prehistoric landscapes from the Cretaceous Period.

They reveal the Flipside.

Now, thirty years after the first Turn, the clockwork is breaking down as one of the world's powers has decided to exploit the phenomenon for their own gain, possibly destroying everything then and now in the process.

A MAN OUT OF TIME
by Christopher Laflan

Five years after the Chinese Axis detonated an unknown weapon of mass destruction off the southern coast of the United States, Special Ops Sergeant John Crider and the members of Shadow Company have finally captured what they all hope will lead to the end of the war. Unfortunately, the population within the United States is no longer sustainable. In an effort to stabilize the economy, the government enacts the Cryonics Act. One hundred years in suspended animation, all debt forgiven, and a chance at a less crowded future are too good to pass up for John and his young daughter.

Except not everything always goes as planned as Sergeant John Crider finds himself pitted against a land of prehistoric monsters genetically resurrected from the fossil record, murderous inhabitants, and a future he never wanted.

SEVEREDPRESS

CHECK OUT OTHER GREAT DINOSAUR BOOKS

PRIMORDIA
by **Greig Beck**

Ben Cartwright, former soldier, home to mourn the loss of his father stumbles upon cryptic letters from the past between the author, Arthur Conan Doyle and his great, great grandfather who vanished while exploring the Amazon jungle in 1908.

Amazingly, these letters lead Ben to believe that his ancestor's expedition was the basis for Doyle's fantastical tale of a lost world inhabited by long extinct creatures. As Ben digs some more he finds clues to the whereabouts of a lost notebook that might contain a map to a place that is home to creatures that would rewrite everything known about history, biology and evolution.

But other parties now know about the notebook, and will do anything to obtain it. For Ben and his friends, it becomes a race against time and against ruthless rivals.

In the remotest corners of Venezuela, along winding river trails known only to lost tribes, and through near impenetrable jungle, Ben and his novice team find a forbidden place more terrifying and dangerous than anything they could ever have imagined.

PANGAEA EXILES
by **Jeff Brackett**

Tried and convicted for his crimes, Sean Barrow is sent into temporal exile—banished to a time so far before recorded history that there is no chance that he, or any other criminal sent back, has any chance of altering history.

Now Sean must find a way to survive more than 200 million years in the past, in a world populated by monstrous creatures that would rend him limb from limb if they got the chance. And that's just his fellow prisoners.

The dinosaurs are almost as bad.